"Quick, to the couch," Kyla gasped

She ran through the office to where a startled man stood behind the desk, and grabbed his arm.

"What the hell?" He resisted her pull.

"No time to explain. We'll be killed if you don't do as I say. Lie on top of me on the couch. Pretend we're making love. It's the only way." She summoned all her strength to drag him toward the couch, then managed to upset his balance enough to haul him down. He landed on top of her with a thud that nearly knocked out her breath. His trench coat billowed out, covering her almost completely. *This could work.*

He tried to struggle up, and she grabbed his belt buckle. She heard the outer office door open and rasped into his ear, "They're coming! You have to act like we're doing it." She bumped her hips against his. "They'll shoot us if we can't fool them."

"Aw, hell, somebody *is* coming." He began to get into it, working his pelvis between her legs. Looking down at her with a twinkle in his eye, he murmured, "I just hope you'll respect me in the morning."

Vicki Lewis Thompson says her inspiration for *Fools Rush In* was the idea of "Being at the wrong place at the wrong time." That's certainly what happens to Kyla Finnegan, the heroine of this exciting Temptation novel, when she inadvertently witnesses a murder. Not only does Kyla—with the help of her hero, Pete Beckett—become an expert at dodging the bad guys, she is also a skilled foot massager. Vicki's sister urged her to go for a foot massage as research for the book. Vicki sums up the experience in three words: "It really hurt!"

Books by Vicki Lewis Thompson

HARLEQUIN TEMPTATION

Don't miss any of our special offers. Write to us at the following address for information on our newest releases.

Harlequin Reader Service
P.O. Box 1397, Buffalo, NY 14240
Canadian address: P.O. Box 603,
Fort Erie, Ont. L2A 5X3

FOOLS RUSH IN

VICKI LEWIS THOMPSON

Harlequin Books

TORONTO • NEW YORK • LONDON
AMSTERDAM • PARIS • SYDNEY • HAMBURG
STOCKHOLM • ATHENS • TOKYO • MILAN
MADRID • WARSAW • BUDAPEST • AUCKLAND

For Shirley Schodtler and Marilyn and John Kudjer,
three of the finest in-laws a girl could have

Published April 1993

ISBN 0-373-25539-X

FOOLS RUSH IN

1

KYLA FINNEGAN had the answer to the world's problems: foot massage.

Apparently Arturo Carmello agreed with her. Kyla smiled as she walked around behind his desk and noticed he'd already removed his socks and shoes. "Looking forward to our session, Mr. Carmello?"

"I tell you, young lady, these foot massages have made a new man of me." He swiveled his executive chair toward her. "I don't know how it works, but it works."

"Think of your feet as a switchboard." Kyla put down her case containing massage oils and a tape recorder. Then she dropped a floor pillow in front of him and sat on it. "I manipulate certain areas of your feet, and a signal goes to a corresponding area of your body." She shrugged out of her quilted jacket and pushed a button on the tape recorder. Soft synthesizer music settled around them.

"Ah." Arturo leaned back and closed his eyes. "There's my angel music."

Kyla smiled. He was such a nice old guy. She found the rumors of his underworld connections hard to believe. After taking a bottle of vanilla-scented oil from her case, she dripped some into her palm.

"That stuff smells great, reminds me of cookies baking. Better than flowery junk."

"I like it, too." Kyla rubbed the oil into her hands and worked on his feet, leaning the ball of each foot over her knuckles.

Arturo sighed, making his round stomach rise and fall like a bellows. "You know, it's not good, you being here after five, then taking the bus home. It gets dark so early in the winter. I worry about you, not having a car and all."

"I manage just fine, Mr. Carmello." She smoothed the top of each foot using rhythmic strokes. "Still have some congestion from that cold, don't you?"

"Yeah."

She pressed more firmly. "This will help."

"Yeah, I can feel it already. You're a good girl, Kyla. Remind me of my daughters. Dark hair like them. You even wear it short and fluffy, like my youngest. Except those blue eyes of yours are different. That Irish blood, I guess. My girls are one-hundred-percent Italian. Good girls, all of you."

"Thanks, Mr. Carmello." She poured more oil on her hands and rotated her thumb beneath the big toe of his left foot.

"Anyways, you should have a boyfriend or somebody take you home, these winter nights. Chicago ain't that safe on the streets after dark."

"I'll tell you a secret, Mr. Carmello." She pushed her thumb against the crevice below his pudgy toes.

"Yeah? What's that?"

"I'm a brown belt in karate. I work out every day."

"You're kidding me."

"Nope. My brother and I started when we were little. Back in California. Anytime somebody tries to mug me, they'll be sorry."

Arturo chuckled. "Good for you. Never woulda guessed, a little thing like you."

Being a "little thing" was exactly why Kyla continued her karate training. She planned never to be physically vulnerable again.

Arturo was quiet for a while. "Could you throw me across the room?" he asked finally.

"No, but I could probably disable you, as long as you didn't have a gun."

"My, my. Picture that." Arturo chuckled again.

"So you can stop worrying and start relaxing, Mr. Carmello. This massage isn't going to relieve your tension unless you stop talking and let me do the work."

"Okay." Arturo's stomach heaved again. "Never woulda thought something like this foot rub would make me feel like a million bucks, but I'm getting so's I can hardly wait for you to show up. I've been thinking about making it five nights instead of just three, if that's okay with you."

"That would be fine." She smoothed her thumb down to his instep. "Now just relax."

He did, and the office became quiet except for the gentle flow of the music and the faint sounds of traffic on the street far below. Kyla loved the tranquillity of the empty building. No slamming doors or elevator bells. She and Arturo might be the only two people left in the fifty-story office complex. The scent of vanilla mingled with the tang of lemon furniture polish used on the black walnut desk. She settled into a rhythm and concentrated on transferring her energy to her client.

This office building had become a good source of revenue. Word was spreading that the person to schedule into your lunch hour or coffee break was Kyla Finnegan, Reflexologist. The job suited her need for independence. She could work in jeans and a sweater—her favorite outfit—and she could set her own hours. Arturo was the only after-five client she had, because she was cautious about making appointments, especially with men, at that time. But Arturo had always treated her with respect.

Kyla wasn't sure what first alerted her to something different in the room. Then she heard a creak. Had the door opened? She stopped stroking the side of Arturo's foot to listen. Was that a footstep? The soft, brushing sound might have been her, shifting her weight on the cushion. Probably Arturo's talk about her not being safe on the streets had made her jumpy.

Holding very still, she concentrated on the noises around her, but could hear only the music and Arturo's breathing. Surely she was imagining things. She resumed her rhythm.

And then the sound came again. It *was* footsteps, slow and measured, the steps of someone approaching the desk with great care. She opened her mouth to say something to Arturo, so he wouldn't be caught unawares by the visitor.

A menacing whoosh, followed by a soft thud, stopped her. Arturo's foot jerked in her hand. She glanced up. A perfect hole had appeared in his white shirt, right over his heart, and a red stain spread around it.

She watched in dazed fascination until reality gripped her. Then horror splashed over her like ice water. A roaring sound filled her ears. It couldn't be. No. His foot was still warm. He couldn't be . . . but he was. His chest had stopped moving.

God, no! Not that dear old man! She swallowed the scream that rose in her throat as instinct took over. *Don't move, Kyla.* She held her breath, clenched her muscles against the trembling fear, the urge to run.

Stay balanced and calm. Survive.

"Well, that about does it," said a male voice from just in front of the desk. It was high-pitched, the kind of voice you remember. "Nice of him to be taking a little nap with his music on."

"Is he dead?" said another man whose voice was deeper.

"He ain't breathing, is he?"

Kyla thought she'd faint. She fought the greenish-black haze that threatened to engulf her. Two men had just shot Arturo Carmello. Shot him while she was holding his foot. And the men didn't know she was there.

DOWN THE HALL and around the corner from Arturo Carmello's office, Pete Beckett opened a file drawer and searched through the contents. He wore gloves. Probably a silly precaution, he thought, but he wasn't supposed to be here, wouldn't be here if it weren't for Peggy. His twin sister had married a jerk, and now she thought he was investing drug money for the mob, Arturo Carmello to be exact.

In the pocket of his tan trench coat was the office key Peggy had mailed to him, enclosed in a letter begging for help. She'd tried to ask her husband about his dealings with Carmello, but Jerald wouldn't talk to her. Peggy was desperate for information, but afraid to hire someone, in case doing that would bring more danger to her family. She didn't know enough about investments to snoop through the files herself. So here was Pete, partner in the respected Minneapolis accounting firm of Beckett and Stripley, playing private eye for his sister.

He scanned the folders, running his gloved index finger down the tabs. He had to admit that the clues Peggy had picked up justified her worst fears. Jerald had been preoccupied and secretive about a promising new account, and she'd overheard him on the phone talking to someone named Art about an investment group called the Aries Consortium. She'd distinctly heard him say, "Don't worry, Art, it can't be traced to you."

Pete pulled the Aries file and opened it. As he scanned the contents, he let out a low whistle. He had a general idea of Jerald's annual income. An account such as this would double it. If the Aries Consortium were legit, Jerald would have bragged to his wife and anyone who'd listen about his newest client. Pete's jaw tightened. This would have to stop.

KYLA HELD HER BREATH. Maybe she could wait them out.

The man with the deeper voice spoke again. "Vinnie, I gotta use the can. I'll bet there's one in this office somewheres."

So the one with the high voice is Vinnie. Then Kyla tried to erase the information. She didn't want to remember anything about the two men.

"Forget that," squeaked Vinnie. "We gotta leave."

"Then leave. I'm looking around. What difference does it make? We got lotsa time. The real janitors won't show up for another two hours."

Kyla knew where the bathroom was. Through a side door was a conference room, and the bathroom was at the far end of it. She used it every time she was here to wash the massage oil from her hands.

"Come on, Vinnie. Check out the place. Pretty plush." The man's voice grew fainter. Kyla guessed he was already in the conference room. "Hey, Vinnie, come in here and see these paintings. More Remingtons, just the kind you like, with cowboys and cows and all that."

"I shouldn'ta brought you on this job, Dominic. You was always too nosy, even when we was kids." His voice, too, became fainter.

Kyla remembered the Remington bronze on the credenza behind her. Once Vinnie started looking, he might want to examine that, too. She had to get out of here. They were both in the other room. She could make it out before they came back. Had to get away. Had to.

She crawled around the desk, careful to make no sound. She wobbled to her feet. There stood Vinnie with his back to her, wearing a janitor's uniform. Balding and skinny, he had ears that stuck straight out. He stared up at a large painting on the conference room wall. Hearing a toilet flush, she ran for the outer office. On the way, her foot caught a metal wastebasket. It rang like a gong.

"Hey!" squealed Vinnie.

She jerked open the outer door and sprinted down the darkened hallway, knowing he must be chasing her. She turned left down an adjoining hall. The translucent glass of one office door shone faintly. Maybe someone was there. She made for the door, panting, praying it would be open. It was. Jerald T. Johnson, Financial Consultant. *Be a hero, Jerry.*

She tore through the deserted outer office into the one marked Jerald T. Johnson. A startled man wearing a trench coat stood behind the desk. She took a quick inventory of the office and could think of only one way out of this. "Quick, to the couch," she gasped, running around the desk and grabbing his arm.

"What the hell?" He resisted her pull.

"No time to explain. We'll be killed if you don't do as I say. Lie on top of me on the couch. Cover me as much as you can. Pretend we're making love. It's the only way."

"You're crazy."

"I'm telling you it's the only way!" She summoned all her strength to drag him toward the couch.

"Look, I don't know what you're up to, but I'm not doing it."

She was out of position for a good flip, but she managed to upset his balance enough to haul him down to the couch. He landed on top of her with a thud that nearly knocked out her breath. He was a good foot taller than she was. Being small helped this time. The trench coat billowed out, covering her almost completely. This could work. This could really work.

He tried to struggle up and she grabbed his belt buckle. She heard the outer office door open and she began to moan. "Oh, Jerry. You're so good, Jerry!"

The man struggled harder. "I'm not—"

"They're coming!" she breathed into his ear. "You have to act like we're doing it." She bumped her hips against his. "They'll shoot us if we can't fool them."

"Aw, hell, somebody *is* coming." He began to get into it, working his pelvis between her legs and pumping up and down. "I hope you'll respect me in the morning." His breathing grew more rapid and he managed a couple of convincing groans.

"Yes!" Kyla cried. "That's it. Right there. Oh, Jerry, Jerry!"

The man pumped faster. His cheek lay against hers, its faint bristle prickly on her skin. The spicy scent of his cologne, warmed by his activity, seeped around her. His lips moved against her earlobe, nibbling. "How's this?" he murmured.

"Good!" she cried, moving upward to meet his thrusts. "Jerry, I love you, love you. Oh!" She began to suspect the guy had an erection. She didn't care. Her heart hammered in her chest as the footsteps came closer and stopped.

"Look at that," squeaked Vinnie from the doorway. "The boss gettin' it on with his secretary."

The man on top of Kyla spoke, his voice seemingly roughened by passion. "You guys are way too early. Get out of here. Now."

Vinnie laughed. "Yeah, we're runnin' ahead of schedule. We can come back when youse is through." The footsteps started out and paused.

Kyla held her breath.

"Do her once for me," Vinnie said. Then he laughed again and walked away. The outer office door closed.

Kyla waited, not moving.

"Janitors," the man said, still breathing hard. "They weren't supposed to come on duty until seven."

"They aren't janitors," she whispered.

"Sure sounded like it to me." He started to get up. "I have to—"

She jerked him back down by his belt buckle. "They have guns. They already killed somebody."

He raised up enough to look into her face. His brown eyes were dark with impatience. "Let go of my belt."

She did.

He levered himself from the couch and started toward the outer office.

"Don't you dare go out there without a weapon."

He paused and glanced at her.

"I'm telling you they have guns."

He sighed and shook his head. Then, moving with a stealth that surprised her, considering he seemed to be your average businessman, he reached for an empty coatrack. Holding it over his shoulder like a baseball bat, he stepped through the door into the outer office.

She held her breath. No shots. Maybe the ruse had worked. Maybe she'd found herself a hero, after all.

Jerry was turning out to be a manly kind of guy. She hated to think what might have happened to her if he hadn't been around. The immediate danger gone, she began to shake. She sat up and hugged herself to stop the trembling. Poor man. The underworld rumors must have been true.

To get her thoughts away from Arturo, she glanced around the office. On the desk was a picture of a dark-haired woman holding two brunette children, both girls. Her hero was married. The woman was very attractive and a good match for Jerry; she could easily have been his sister.

Jerry's wife was a lucky woman, Kyla decided. Her husband had solid good looks—trim build, dark hair combed back from a nice widow's peak, strong features. All that and courage, too.

Kyla continued her survey of the room. Anything was better than thinking about Arturo and the two men with guns. Jerry liked candid photos, apparently. The walls were covered with shots of various people, but she found only one of him with his wife. They were standing on a sailboat, arms casually around each other's shoulders, and Jerry had his shirt off. Nice chest. Kyla had always been partial to a little chest hair.

Jerry came back into the office and stood the coatrack in its proper place. "They seem to be gone. I locked the outer office door. Should have done it before."

If he had, she'd be dead. Kyla stood on rubbery legs and prayed they'd hold her. "If they decide to come back, I doubt if a locked door will stop them. We need to leave."

He sighed and shoved his hands into his coat pockets. "Okay, lay it on me. What supposedly happened to send you racing in here?"

"Those guys disguised themselves as janitors, walked into an office down the hall and . . ." The scene came back to her and she felt bubbles of hysteria rising under her layer of calm. She stared at the snowy white blotter on the desk until she'd blanked out the scene. "They shot somebody," she recited, pretending she was reading lines from a play. "He's dead. I saw them do it."

He stared at her. "Who did they shoot?"

"Arturo Carmello."

Jerry paled. "Oh, God."

"You knew him?"

He shook his head. "I've heard of him."

"Listen, I'm not kidding. I'm grateful for what you've done so far, but we need to get out of here. We—" She reached for her jacket and remembered where it was. "Damn!"

"What?"

She struggled against panic. "I left my stuff back in Arturo's office. My massage oils, my tape recorder, my jacket—with my wallet and keys in the pocket—dammit! This is terrible. Just terrible." She felt invaded, defiled. She wanted to scream, but didn't dare make a noise that would draw attention back to this office. Gritting her teeth, she began to pace. "Those guys will know who I am, where I live. They'll have a key to get in my apartment. They'll—"

"Massage oil? You were giving Carmello a massage?"

She stopped pacing and glared at him. Sure enough, he was looking at her as if she were some sort of floozy. She'd run into the reaction before. "Foot massage," she said, anger making her response choppy. "I'm a licensed reflexologist."

"A what?"

She was used to that, too. People in the Midwest weren't as familiar with the technique as they'd been in California, which was one reason she'd relocated—less competition. "Never mind." She wasn't about to explain anything at this point. "Listen, let's just get out of here, Jerry. Maybe we fooled those guys. Maybe not. Maybe they'll rethink the whole thing and come back. Do you have a car?"

"Yes."

"Good. Much better than a cab. Let's go." She started toward the outer office.

"Before we do that, maybe you should know something."

She turned. "What now?"

"My name's not Jerry."

2

KYLA STOPPED. "Then who are you? And what are you doing in this office? With gloves on, come to think of it."

"I'd rather not say right now. Still want to ride off into the night with me?"

Kyla looked at the picture on the wall, of two people standing on a boat—this man and the woman who was also in the desktop picture with the two little girls. "If you're not Jerald T. Johnson, what are you doing in a picture with his wife?"

"I think it's time we got out of here, don't you?" He closed a folder on the desk and replaced it in an open file drawer. "Or would you rather stick around and discuss this until those guys, whoever they are, show up again?" He shoved the file drawer and it rumbled back into place.

She watched him adjust everything on the desk. He looked uneasy. "I think I get it. You don't want to be caught here, either."

He glanced up from the desk. "Let's just say it's your turn to trust me."

Kyla debated. She remembered the solid feel of this not-Jerald T. Johnson man as he'd lain on top of her. She remembered that he'd set out to face men with guns, while armed with only a coatrack. Maybe he was a mobster, too. Maybe they were all mobsters. But Arturo would have protected her if he could have. And this guy seemed to be temporarily on her side. She couldn't afford to be choosy, and she still had her karate. It would keep her safe as long as she didn't have to deal with guns. Again.

"Ready?" he asked, lifting one dark eyebrow.

Kyla thought about her coat. She hated losing it, not to mention her tape recorder and massage oils, but only a fool would return to that office and take a chance the killers were lying in wait. Most likely they'd already confiscated her stuff and were on their way to her apartment. She sighed. "Let's go."

Johnson and Carmello both had offices on the thirty-fifth floor. Kyla suggested taking the elevator to the underground parking garage. It was a more visible means of escape, but faster than climbing down thirty-five flights. "Besides, if they found my coat, they've probably already left," she said as they stepped into the fume-filled garage.

The man paused and put out his arm, as if to hold her back while he checked around. She appreciated that. "I don't see anything suspicious," he said.

"Me, neither." Kyla tried not to shiver as the cold sliced through her cable-knit sweater.

"The car's over there." He pointed to a red compact. "Stick close."

"Right." Kyla hugged herself as they started toward the car. Then she noticed the sticker on the bumper. "A rental?" Her teeth chattered in spite of herself. "Is yours in the shop, or are you f-from out of t-town?"

"Are you cold or scared?"

Both, mister. "Cold," she said aloud. She wasn't in the habit of admitting fear to a stranger.

"Take my coat." Shrugging out of his trench coat, he lifted it to her shoulders.

"No, thanks. I'm fine."

He stopped in mid-motion, looked at her, and finally pulled his coat back on and tied the belt. "Tough little cookie, aren't you?"

"Yes, and you didn't answer my question about the rental car."

He unlocked her door without comment.

"Tough big cookie, aren't you?"

He gave her a wry smile before closing the door.

She waited until he'd rounded the car and slid into the driver's seat. "I'm not supposed to ask questions, is that right?"

"That's right." He turned the key in the ignition and backed out of the parking space.

As they approached the parking garage exit, which funneled traffic out onto Michigan Avenue, Kyla wondered if the killers would be out there, ready to shoot them. "Hunch down," she warned as they neared the opening.

"Somebody has to drive."

"But—"

"I'm not negotiating rush-hour traffic in a crouch."

"Okay." She steeled herself when they emerged from the exit and blended with the other northbound cars. Something pelted the car and she cried out.

"Rain." He switched on the wipers.

"Oh. Yeah." She felt really dumb. "Look, I'm not one of those scaredy-cat women."

"Good for you." He guided the car with ease. Flicking his gaze over her huddled form, he turned on the heater. James Bond himself couldn't have been more maddeningly calm in a crisis.

She wondered if he was a mobster, after all. He seemed to take all this in stride. She felt the urge to defend herself. "It's just that I'm not used to guns and killing. It may be commonplace for you, in your line of work, whatever that is, looking through files with gloves on and everything."

He responded with a humorless chuckle that made her feel even more inadequate. She decided to stop apologizing. She'd done the best she could under the circumstances. As warm air wrapped around her, she relaxed enough to look out the window.

Heavy traffic flowed through the canyon of skyscrapers, and a chorus of honking horns echoed against the granite walls. Kyla wondered if anyone heard the horns; most people were hooked up to Walkmans or cellular telephones. A bus roared past and screeched to a halt at the intersection. Taxis vied for the business of those who could afford them. The mass of humanity struggling to get home or to the nearest restaurant made a good camouflage.

Kyla began to believe they'd really escaped. She took a deep breath and turned to her escort. "Where are we going?"

"You tell me. I suggest dropping you off at the nearest police station."

The fear, never quite erased, returned in a rush. "No!"

"No? Unless you made up that story back there, you just witnessed a serious crime. I think they'd like to know about it."

"Oh, I'm sure they would. I'm sure they'd like to make me a star witness. You know what happens to people who step forward in a killing like this?"

"They're called good citizens."

"They're called chumps. Because they get what's coming to them." She sliced a finger across her neck.

"The police have some sort of witness protection program, don't they? They'd keep you safe."

Kyla glanced at him in disdain. "Obviously you don't have much experience with the police."

"And you do?"

"Let's just say that they can't always keep you safe." A vision appeared in her mind of her stepfather battering down the front door when she was five years old. She trembled. Old memories. This man wouldn't understand. "I'm not going to the police. If you drop me off there, I'll run away, take my chances hiding out on my own." She watched his face for signs that he was considering dumping her out somewhere. A tightening of his jaw, a compression of his lips would mean he'd made that sort of decision.

Instead he frowned, as if thinking of alternatives.

Kyla gained confidence. Her instincts had been on target. He would help her if he could.

At last he glanced at her. "Obviously you can't go home, if it's true that they have your address and a key to get in."

"Obviously."

"I assume you don't have a roommate or you'd have mentioned it."

"That's right. No roommate."

"Boyfriend?"

"No."

He was silent for an excruciatingly long time. Finally he spoke. "Where do you want to go?"

She decided two could play the waiting game, and besides, she was still thinking. She watched a droplet of rain escape the wipers. Pushed by wind resistance, it raced up the windshield in a sparkling ascent. They'd reached Wacker Drive. The man turned right, following the Chicago River toward Lake Michigan. "Where are you going?"

"Back to my hotel."

A lakefront hotel. Ritzy. She'd expect that from a mobster. "So you *are* from out of town."

He didn't answer.

"Take me with you to the hotel."

He paused a beat. "You're kidding."

"Just for now." The pavement, glistening like wet sealskin, reflected the silver and crimson shine of headlights and taillights. "I have to have time to think, decide what to do."

"I have no idea who you are, two guys may be out to kill you, and you want to stay in my hotel room?"

She looked at him without flinching. "Yes."

"Why should I agree to that? You could be making all of this up. You could be working some shakedown of your own, with me as the intended victim."

"Do I seem like that sort of person?"

He stopped at a red light and surveyed her. "Yep."

"Well, I'm not. You have nothing to fear from me."

"So you say. Look, there's a patrol car. I'll just wave it over and—"

"Don't you dare!"

"Why not?"

She thought fast. "If you signal that police car I'll tell them how I got away, and the man I was with, and where I found him. They might be interested in why a man wearing gloves was going over the accounts in Jerald T. Johnson's office."

He gripped the steering wheel more tightly. "I see."

"The one thing you should remember about me is that I'm a survivor, Mr. Whoever-you-are."

He sighed. "I can believe it. You'll probably outlast me." He hesitated, and finally spoke in a resigned tone. "Okay. We'll go to my hotel room. I'll have to take my chances that you won't steal everything I own, but you're not staying long. You'll have to find some other place to hide out, or whatever it is you're doing."

Kyla didn't answer. She had no other place, or people to count on, now that her brother Trevor was on an aircraft carrier somewhere in the Pacific. So far this man was her best bet. The good thing was, he didn't want to talk to the police any more than she did. She'd love to know why. Maybe she'd get the truth out of him yet.

He pulled the car onto Lake Shore Drive and they passed the green security lights of Navy Pier. Yes, he was definitely headed for one of the new luxury hotels on the lake. She wished she could look forward to the experience of staying in such a nice place. Maybe things would be better if she could become friends with this man. The first step was to learn his name.

She started out bravely. "Since we'll be together for a while—"

"A very short while."

Maybe they couldn't be friends. She retreated into her shell. "Whatever. I'd still like to know what I can call you. Unless you want me to keep on using Jerry."

"No, thanks. You can call me Pete."

"Is that your real name?"

"Yes."

"I'm Kyla Finnegan, although you never bothered to ask."

"Because I didn't want to know. I have a feeling the less I know about you, the better."

Kyla had exactly the opposite plan with Pete. The more she knew about him, the better. Friendly or not, he was her one hope until her brother Trevor came home on leave in three days.

WHAT A MESS, Pete thought as he swung the rental car into the underground parking garage beneath the hotel. All his life he'd walked the straight and narrow, never doing anything remotely outside the law, except the time he spray-painted the water tower a week before high school graduation. A woman had dragged him into that, too—his steady girl Janene, who'd suggested the best way to prove his love was to spray-paint her name on the tower. He'd felt like a hero until someone on the school board figured out who the tower artist was and threatened to pull his diploma. So much for wild and crazy.

Until tonight. He hadn't been able to refuse Peggy's hysterical pleas, but he'd counted on her suspicions being wrong. Just his luck they were right on target. Now it looked as if he and Peggy would have to confront his brother-in-law. Peggy didn't want to leave him. Jerald was an okay father and the girls seemed to love him. Peggy did, too, although he couldn't fathom why.

Pete had no idea how Jerald would react to the news that his brother-in-law had snooped through his files. He might try to ruin Pete's career; he'd always been a vindictive sonofabitch. If he now had connections with the underworld, he was even more dangerous.

And this woman who had supposedly witnessed the murder of Arturo Carmello—was she a poor kid caught in a bad situation or an experienced con artist? Whichever she was, she was smart enough to use his vulnerability to get her way. He couldn't let Jerald find out about his nocturnal activities yet. First he had to talk to Peggy, think this thing through, find out if Arturo Carmello was really dead.

He parked in an available slot and pulled on the emergency brake. Too bad there didn't seem to be one for his life.

"This is a very nice hotel." Her voice seemed smaller, more subdued.

"My sister is—" He caught himself just in time. He'd been about to say that his sister was paying for his stay. He didn't really have the hang of this cloak-and-dagger stuff.

"Your sister is what? The manager or something?"

He glanced at her. "No, she's not." In the dim light of the parking garage her eyes seemed enormous. He remembered how blue they were in the light. He remembered some other things, too. The scent of vanilla, the softness of her breasts, the jolt of sexual excitement when she'd pushed up against him, spread her legs and urged him on. He was a little embarrassed that he'd responded so quickly.

At least she'd had the decency to ignore his obvious arousal. He could still hear, plain as day, her cries of passion. Faked, of course. Lillian, the woman he was going to marry, was a silent lover. Pete hadn't realized until tonight how much that bugged him. This gamine creature's moans, bogus or not, had turned him on in a way he hadn't been turned on in a long time.

"What's the matter?" She sounded nervous, wary.

"Nothing." He reached for the door handle. "Let's go upstairs."

"Um, you offered your coat before. Could I wear it now? Maybe if I turn the collar up and we hurry through the lobby, people won't have much chance to notice me."

He glanced at her and laughed. "If anything, you'll attract more attention that way. You'll look like a motorized trench coat."

A dimple appeared at the corner of her mouth. "Okay, so I'll look silly, but those guys saw what I'm wearing. I'd like to cover it up, just in case they have some sort of underworld spy network."

He registered the appeal of that dimple. *Easy does it, Beckett.* Striving for bored nonchalance, he shrugged. "Your choice." If she wore his trench coat into the lobby, people might think he was smuggling a call girl up to his room. For all he knew, he was. He got out of the car, took off his coat and held it while she slipped her arms into the sleeves. As he'd expected, the coat reached to her toes. If she was much over five feet tall, he'd be amazed.

As she stood there belting the coat and pulling the collar around her face, she looked small and brave. He had the insane urge to put his arms around her and protect her from the world. He must be losing it. She was already using a form of extortion to procure his help. He'd said it himself: she was a tough little cookie. And yet, walking along in that giant trench coat, she looked more like a lost waif. Refusing to analyze further his unsettling reaction to her, he reminded himself that feeling anything for this woman could be dangerous to his health.

DOMINIC DROVE THE CAR, his beefy hands dwarfing the wheel, while his partner gave directions. Vinnie didn't need a map to find Kyla Finnegan's address. He knew Chicago inside out. Her wallet was in his hand and her apartment key was in his pocket, but the rest of her stuff—her coat, massage oils, tape recorder and pillow—was hidden in the trunk.

"Turn left here," he said. "And don't squeal the tires! This ain't no gangster movie. Some cop might hear and come take a look-see."

"If you'd tell me the address, I wouldn't *hafta* squeal the tires, cousin. You never tell me nothin'."

"I tell you what you need to know."

"Well, I know we gotta get to her place before she does." Dominic's tone was belligerent.

"We will. She don't have no driver's license, so she has to take the bus."

"No license? How'd you know her address?"

"Library card. Slow down. We're coming up on it. There. Number 622. Apartment B. She's in the top flat. Good thing it's a neighborhood like this, and not some high security apartment house."

"Remember that two-flat place we lived in when we was kids? Down in the old neighborhood? You and your ma on the top floor, me and my folks on the bottom. We musta been what?—five and eight."

Vinnie looked at him. "Sometimes I think youse is still five, Dominic. Park between them two cars. We're going in." He inspected the house as Dominic backed the sedan into a parallel parking slot.

"Hey, Vinnie, what're we gonna do with her oils and stuff?"

"We'll dump 'em in the lake when we dump her in." Lights shone from the windows of the first floor, but the top floor was dark. There was an outside entrance and stairs up to the door into the second flat. He'd been in a hundred buildings just like this one.

"I was thinkin' I'd take some of that oil back to Suzanne, you know? I always wanted her to learn massage. I'd like—"

"Dominic, if you don't stop flippin' your lip, I'm gonna put you in the trunk, too. Let's go."

At the top of the inside stairs, Vinnie paused. "Ring the bell. She might have a roommate or somethin'."

Dominic pushed the button twice while Vinnie fidgeted with the keys and glanced down the stairs behind them.

Finally Vinnie shoved the keys at Dominic. "Nobody's in there. You go first." He waited until the door swung open and Dominic groped his way inside before he stepped in himself and closed the door. He waited for his eyes to adjust to the light, but Dominic was stumbling all around, falling against things.

"Can't find a lamp," Dominic muttered.

"Idiot! Don't turn on no lights until we close the curtains. We don't—"

Dominic yelled and something inhuman screeched.

Vinnie whirled and reached for his gun. "What the hell was that?"

"Cat. I musta tripped over it. Damn, I can't see nothin'. How about that little flashlight that you—"

"Find the cord for the curtains, damn youse! If she comes home, we don't want her to know we're here, do we?" Vinnie retreated to the front door and patted the wall for the light switch. When he heard the swish of curtains being pulled across the front window, he turned on the switch.

"That's better," Dominic said, mopping his face with a handkerchief. "Youse know I'm scared of the dark."

Vinnie glanced around. "Reflexologists must not make much dough. She don't have hardly any furniture or nothin'."

"You just don't like this place 'cause it's got that whadyacallit New Age stuff in here. Peace posters and dolphins, and like that. Incense. I think it's kinda nice. And I like the cat, too. Wonder where it went? Here, kitty, kitty."

Vinnie sighed. "Sometimes I don't think you take things serious, Dominic."

"Sure I do." Dominic wandered into the small kitchen.

Vinnie heard a rattling sound like something being poured into a plastic dish. "Dominic, for God's sake! Are you feeding that damned cat?"

Dominic appeared in the kitchen doorway. "You know something? This cat's got no tail."

"As if I care."

A gray cat appeared in the kitchen doorway and wound itself through Dominic's thick legs. "See? It's getting used to me." A soft purr came from the cat and it butted its head against his shin. "See? It likes me."

"Ain't that wonderful."

"Animals always like me. It's a gift. I shoulda been a vet."

Vinnie grimaced. "That's for sure. Then we wouldn't be having this problem locatin' a witness." He went to the living room window, parted the curtain slightly and looked out.

"That's not fair. It's not only my fault. If we'd left that office right away you woulda missed that girl completely."

"And she wouldn't have seen us, neither."

"How d'ya know she did?"

Vinnie let the curtain fall and turned back to Dominic. "I was standing in the goddamned door, waiting for you to come out of the can. She seen me all right."

"But not me, right, Vinnie?"

"Look, it don't matter, okay? She seen me, she might as well have seen the both of us. The cops finger me, I finger you."

"Aw, Vinnie."

"Remember that, Dominic. Just in case you think of runnin' out on me, just in case you think you're not gonna be the one to take care of this girl."

"But I ain't never done a girl before."

"Then it's about time. Practice on the cat."

"Vinnie!" Dominic crouched and stroked the cat. "I'm gonna take it home."

"Use what little brains you've got. You take her cat home, a kind with no tail, and some jerk could recognize it. Slip-ups—like us not knowing about this girl being in the office after hours—that's what can put you away. You wouldn't like jail, Dominic."

Dominic didn't answer. He reached inside his jacket, took the gun from his shoulder holster and pointed it at the cat's head. "Bang," he whispered.

STILL WEARING Pete's trench coat, Kyla stood in the middle of the large suite and looked around. A crystal bowl of magenta and white carnations sat on the coffee table in front of a white brocade sofa. Two wing chairs upholstered in burgundy flanked the sofa. Against the opposite wall stood a polished wood armoire that probably contained a television. To her right were a wet bar and a Queen Anne-style desk; to her left were the bedroom and bath. As she'd suspected earlier, she hadn't attached herself to a pauper.

She glanced in his direction. He was heading toward the bedroom.

"I have to make a phone call," he explained.

"A phone call?" Her heart pounded. He was turning her in.

"Don't look like that. This has nothing to do with you." He walked into the bedroom and closed the door.

"Like I'm going to believe you," she muttered. She took off the coat and draped it over the arm of a wing-back before crossing to the bedroom door and placing her ear against it. Years of listening to her parents to gauge the next approaching fight had made her an excellent eavesdropper.

" . . . been doing business with Carmello," Pete said to whoever he was calling. "But I want you to watch the news tonight. It's possible Carmello's been shot. He might be dead."

Kyla held her breath. If he planned to turn her in, now would be the moment.

"Never mind how I know."

Kyla let out her breath.

"Good God, Peggy!" Pete cried, loud enough that she'd have been able to hear him without plastering her ear to the door. "Sure I want to help you and the girls, but that doesn't include murdering somebody. How could you say that?"

Peggy and the girls. Kyla tried to imagine who they might be. A madam and her prostitutes. He'd made some reference to his sister. His sister was a madam! It had to be something like that, something illegitimate, for him to be so secretive. She pictured a high-class operation that brought in thousands of dollars. If Pete could afford a room in this hotel, he might be some sort of business manager for them. Or maybe Jerald T. Johnson was. Maybe—

The door flew open and she nearly fell into the room.

Pete glared down at her. "I thought I heard someone gasp."

She glanced past him. The phone was in its cradle. While she'd been by the door spinning her theories, the conversation had ended.

She lifted her chin and returned his glare. "I have a right to know who I'm mixed up with."

"Who says?"

"I do. Besides, what difference does it make if I know your sister manages a house of prostitution? You think I'll go running to the police to report—"

"House of prostitution? How in the hell did you come up with that?"

"Logical deduction. You said you wanted to help her and the girls. Peggy is your sister, right?"

He didn't answer.

"Never mind. I know she is. So you're helping her manage her, uh, establishment, and Jerald T. Johnson is a pimp who is—was—doing business with Carmello. How'm I doing?"

"Lousy." He sighed. "Maybe telling you the truth is less dangerous than letting your imagination go into overdrive. No telling what could happen if you're operating on the assumption that my twin sister runs a whorehouse."

Kyla folded her arms and smiled. At least she'd get her explanation. "Twins, huh?"

"Yes. My sister is a society wife married to Jerald T. Johnson, who is an investment counselor, not a pimp." The corner of his mouth twitched into a frown. "Although sometimes, I— Well, anyway, that's not important. What is important is that Peggy thinks Jerald was doing business with Carmello. The 'girls' you thought were prostitutes are my nieces, ages seven and nine."

"Oh." She thought about the pictures she'd seen in the office. "That explains a lot. You were snooping around for your sister, then?"

"I was trying to get evidence, so I could confront Jerald with some facts, maybe scare him into giving up his dealings with Carmello."

A new hope dawned within her. "Are you some sort of private eye?"

"A CPA."

"Oh." Her shoulders sagged with disappointment. A private eye might know how to get her out of this tangle without involving the police. But at least this guy was loyal to his sister. Her brother Trevor would do the same kind of thing for her, if she asked him. Just as she'd do anything for Trevor. She'd protected him from their stepfather when he was little, helped him decide what to do with his life, stored his few belongings in her apartment. She'd even—

Oh, no. How could she have forgotten? Something had to be done right away.

"What is it?" He peered down at her. "Kyla, your face is white. Is something wrong?"

"Something sure is wrong." She glanced up at him, wondering if he could be part of the solution. "In all the excitement, I completely forgot about Sex."

3

SHE'S CRAZY, Pete thought. Or else *she's* a hooker. She'd come up with those realistic moans pretty fast when they were on the office couch together. Maybe that explained her theory that Peggy and the girls were prostitutes—she was used to that life. Hadn't she been giving Carmello a massage? And now that she was here, she thought he'd expect sex from her. Which of course he wouldn't, even though he kept wanting to reach out and touch her. He didn't know why that was. Lillian—tall, blond and willowy, sophisticated and aloof—was his type, not this munchkin.

"Look, I'm not sure what kind of guy you think I am," he began, guiding her away from the bedroom toward the brocade sofa as much for his own peace of mind as hers. That episode in Jerald's office had been a tease of an experience, and now he couldn't help wondering what the real thing would be like.

Nevertheless, that wouldn't be appropriate, or fair to Lillian, for that matter. And here he was touching Kyla again. He released her arm and sat down on the sofa. "I'm not planning to...have sex with you." He had trouble saying the last part. It rang in his ears with unnatural urgency. *Have sex with you... have sex with you.* He felt the beginning twitches of desire.

"What?" She looked blank at first, and then she began to laugh. "Oh, I didn't mean that kind of sex." She sat down not far from him.

"Or kinky stuff, either." The more he denied his interest, the more the idea appealed to him. She was grinning at him, no doubt amused at his reluctance. Beneath her sweater and jeans her compact little body suggested all sorts of delights to him. Maybe he was a fool to pass up such a chance. "Kyla, I think—"

"Sex is a cat."

His forehead creased. "A cat?"

Kyla nodded, still smiling. "My brother's cat. He saw a letter in Dear Abby about a guy who had a dog named Sex. That gave Trevor the idea to name his cat Sex Kitten, Sex for short. I'm so used to her name that I don't think about it any more. I forget that other people will assume . . . well, what you assumed."

"Your brother has a cat named Sex." Pete found he was deeply disappointed that she wasn't propositioning him. He was also confused. "So what's that got to do with anything?"

"Trevor's in the navy and I'm taking care of Sex...of his cat."

Pete was having a hard time keeping his libido in check with this kind of talk. He forced his expression into an impassive mask. "So your brother's cat is in your apartment?"

"Yes. And we have to get her out of there."

He stared at her. His first assessment had been correct. She was crazy. "Isn't this the same apartment with killers lurking around? Killers who even have a key to the place?"

She threw back her shoulders, which thrust her breasts into sharp relief against the white fabric of her sweater. "I don't care."

He was beginning to care about all the wrong things.

"That cat is my responsibility," she continued. "Those two men might hurt her. She won't get food and water for who knows how long. She's an innocent bystander who doesn't understand what's going on. I'm not about to let that cat suffer." She studied him. "You figured out how to get into Jerald T. Johnson's office without being caught. You can probably help me figure this out, too."

"Oh, no." He edged away from her on the couch. "You're not dragging me into this. This is a cat we're talking about, not a human being."

Her blue eyes flashed. "Sex is better than most people I know!"

Pete had a hard time keeping a straight face. This was funny, but damned stimulating, too. He liked her passionate intensity. He couldn't help comparing her spirited approach to Lillian's cool poise. He'd been attracted to Lillian because he'd believed that still waters ran deep. He'd been waiting, he now realized, for her to reveal her fiery depths. Maybe Lillian didn't have fiery depths. Maybe sometimes still waters were just stagnant.

With an effort he brought his mind back to the problem at hand. "What if you called and asked somebody to check on the cat, maybe take her home with them?"

"I most certainly will not." Her look was indignant. "I could be sending someone in to meet a couple of killers."

"Oh. Right." He was so preoccupied with her that he wasn't thinking straight.

"And what if the killers have Sex right this minute?"

He couldn't help laughing. God, she was appealing. "That would be interesting."

"Oh, for heaven's sake!"

"I'd have to be a saint to keep ignoring those lines you throw out." *Or to ignore how vibrant you are, or the hints of how passionate you could be with the right man…with me. Oh, Kyla, I'm in trouble.* "Don't blame me. You're the one with the cat named Sex." *And the bluest eyes I've ever seen.*

"Make fun all you want. Knock yourself out. I'm rescuing my brother's cat." She stood.

"Hey, be reasonable." He pushed himself up from the sofa. "A cat is not worth risking your life for."

"Yes, she is. I can't expect you to understand, but she is. Trevor and I never had . . . well, let's say that cat means a lot to Trevor and me. If anything happens to her, if I didn't even try to save her, I'd never forgive myself."

"Kyla—"

"I'm not asking you to go, but it would help a lot if I could borrow your car."

"And then what? Assuming you got the cat, which I doubt you would without getting killed, what happens after that?"

She tapped a finger against her lips. "You're right. Besides, I don't have an Illinois driver's license. Forget the car. I'd better take the bus. If they saw the car, they might trace it back to you."

"To hell with that!" He was amazed that she cared about his welfare and furious that she'd put herself in this kind of danger. And he was sure it would be dangerous; he no longer doubted her story. Somewhere in all the discussion of cats and brothers he'd decided she was telling the truth. "What about you? You're on the run from these guys, hiding out so they won't shoot you, and you're ready to saddle yourself with a cat?"

She put her face closer to his. "I'm getting that cat."

He wondered if anything would distract her. He had the urge to kiss her. To do more than that, if he were honest with himself. Maybe if he made a pass, she'd forget the whole idea of rescuing the cat. Yeah, right. She was going after that animal, no matter what he said or did. He'd only been around her a.couple of hours, and he already knew enough about her to realize that once fixed on a scheme, she wouldn't be dissuaded. "Okay. Supposing you get back to your apartment. Do you even have a plan of how to get the cat out?"

She hesitated.

"Well?"

"Of course I have a plan."

He folded his arms. "This should be good."

"I order a pizza."

"Order a *pizza*? Now you're hungry?"

"No, a pizza for those two guys. That's the decoy. Plus, the doorbell always makes Sex run into my bedroom and hide behind the teddy bear on my dresser. She stays there a couple of minutes before coming out to investigate, so I have just enough time, after I climb in the window, to grab her and get out."

"Climb in the window?" Pete groaned. "This gets worse and worse."

"Now stop that! Show some confidence. Didn't I get us out of the other situation?"

"You out and me in." And he *was* in. He couldn't stop her, and he couldn't let her go alone. Maybe his judgment was being ruled by a part of his body other than his head, but he was going to help her do this. Fool that he was, he was about to play hero.

He considered the consequences. They'd have to bring the cat back here and smuggle it into the hotel. He didn't even want to think about how they'd manage that. Maybe it wouldn't matter. They'd both be shot rescuing the cat.

To his surprise the whole adventure had his adrenaline pumping and he felt more alive than he had in months—no, years. Since he'd spray-painted the water tower. "Don't you lock your bedroom window?"

"Lock's broken. Landlord never fixed it." She looked as if she could read his thoughts, as if she knew she had already won him over.

"And this window is on the ground floor?"

"Second floor, but there's a tree out back. I can climb it."

"Wrong. I'm climbing it."

"That's wonderful of you, Pete, but you're too big for the tree, and the window, for that matter. Besides, Sex doesn't know you. I really appreciate that you'd try, though." Her smile drove the final nail in his coffin. "You can drive the getaway car."

KYLA HAD PUT a lot of effort into seeming confident about her plan to rescue Sex, but less than an hour later as Pete drove the car down her street, her mouth was dry and her hands shook. They'd agreed to cruise past the house to make sure the men were in there before they ordered the pizza.

She sat up straighter as they neared the duplex. "That's it, third on the left, number 622."

"Can you tell anything?"

"No . . . wait, yes." Her heart hammered, and the beating sound filled her ears. "The curtains are closed in the front room. I always leave them open so Sex can see out. They're in there. God, I hope they haven't hurt her."

"It'll be okay." His voice was steady. "Where's the phone booth?"

"Right up ahead, on the corner." Instead of pointing, Kyla clenched her hands to keep them still. She couldn't let him know how scared she was.

He glanced at her. "You're sure about this?"

"Absolutely sure. I have to get Sex."

He chuckled. "Oh, Kyla."

This time she didn't mind how he'd taken her remark. His soft chuckle sounded reassuring. Jokes were good in a situation like this. Definitely good.

She made the call from memory, as she had countless nights before this. Moments later Pete switched off the headlights and eased the car up the narrow alley behind the row of houses.

Kyla peered ahead. Fear had created a funny lump in her throat. She swallowed. "Don't hit any trash cans."

"Right. How many minutes since we called?"

"Six. It takes them twelve to deliver." She was perspiring under the double layer of sweaters. Pete had loaned her a navy blue one of his to cover her white cable-knit so she wouldn't be so conspicuous in the dark.

"Eat pizza a lot, do you?"

She swallowed again. "Why do you suppose I thought up this idea?"

"Listen, if one of the guys starts back to the bedroom, whether you've got the cat or not, you shimmy down that tree and get your little behind out to this car."

"Pete, I asked you to drive the getaway car. I didn't say you could be in charge."

"Dammit, Kyla—"

"This is it." She unfastened her seat belt and pointed out the driver's side window. "See that break in the fence?"

"I see it."

"I'll get through there. You can see to the street from here. I'll be waiting up in the tree, and when the pizza truck gets here, flash your lights once. I'll count to ten and go in the window. That should be about the time the doorbell rings."

He unbuckled his seat belt. "You seem to be pretty familiar with this kind of situation."

Kyla thought of all the times she'd schemed to outwit her stepfather. Climbing out windows and creating distractions were only a few of the techniques she'd learned. "Like I said, I'm a survivor." She opened the door slowly, making as little noise as possible.

Cold damp air wafted into the car, and she felt like a skydiver poised at the open door of a plane ten thousand feet up. For one moment she wanted to close the door and tell Pete to drive away. But Sex needed her. Trevor would be home on his first leave in three days and the cat had to be there, alive and well.

She turned to Pete. "Wish me luck," she whispered.

Without warning, he leaned over and kissed her on the mouth. The kiss was firm and deliberate. His warm lips packed a sensuous wallop that plunged straight down to the spot where desire stirred within her. He drew back, his dark eyes on her.

"What was that for?" she murmured, startled by the instant response of her body.

He cleared his throat. "Luck."

"Thanks." With one last look into his eyes, she stepped into the muddy alley, where the air didn't feel quite as cold as before she'd been kissed by Pete.

The rain had stopped but clouds still hid the night sky, making the alley darker than usual. About a hundred yards away a dusk-to-dawn light mounted on a pole gave faint illumination, enough for Kyla to make out the break in the fence as she slipped through it into the small backyard. She skirted the rusty clothesline poles and walked across the yard toward the oak tree beside the house. The ground smelled dank and her shoes squished against the wet leaves and soggy grass.

The thumping of her heart and a ringing in her ears made it difficult to hear, but she strained to make out noises. The couple who lived below her, Jen and Donnie Halbertson, had their stereo on—loud heavy metal. That was good. The men wouldn't be able to hear her as well when she climbed through the window. She'd never found much in common with the Halbertsons, but right now she'd give all the money in her checking account to be able to knock on their door and have a neighborly chat about garbage pickup and their stingy landlord who never fixed anything.

But she couldn't knock on the Halbertsons' door, couldn't involve them in this. She wouldn't have involved Pete, except in her desperation, and now it felt nice to have someone willing to help her over the rough spots. Pete was turning out to be a good choice for that. Pete. She touched her still-tingling lips.

The bark of the maple was wet. She grabbed a low-hanging branch, which wouldn't have been there if the landlord believed in trimming trees, and hoisted herself up, scraping her hands in the process. She remembered teaching Trevor to climb trees. As an older sister she'd considered it her responsibility. Bracing her foot between two branches, she moved up another few feet, and another, until she was perched in a crevice right next to her bedroom window.

The climbing had kept her occupied, but now that she was there she had time to think, time to realize she was about to enter an apartment occupied by killers. They'd put a bullet in Arturo Carmello's heart without a thought. They wanted to do the same to her. Now they had Trevor's cat. She couldn't let them hurt her.

But if she didn't stop shaking, she'd fall out of the tree. The ground was a long way down. She looked over the fence to where the rental car sat gleaming dully in the frosty glow from the dusk-to-dawn light. Pete was in there. Pete had kissed her. And she didn't even know his last name.

From out on the street came the sound of an engine and the metallic squeal of brakes. The rental car's lights flashed. Kyla felt as if her chest were clamped in a vise. The pizza was here. She started to count. *Mississippi one, Mississippi two* . . .

Bracing herself against the tree, she reached for the windowsill. With one hand on the sill, she pushed gently on the sash. . . . *Mississippi five, Mississippi six* . . .

The window creaked softly and slid up about five inches. She held her breath, heard nothing except the music downstairs, and pushed it up some more. *Mississippi nine, Mississippi ten.* The doorbell rang. Then came exclamations of surprise, one high-pitched and one low. Sex's claws scratched the oak floor as she skidded down the hall toward the bedroom. What a great sound. Sex was okay. But Kyla had to make her move. Now.

Heart thundering, she shoved the window all the way up and pulled herself across the sill. The sweater snagged on the rough surface. She heard the men arguing. *Open the door. Buy the pizza*, she prayed, wriggling over the sill and easing herself to the floor just as Sex leaped up on the dresser.

"I didn't order no pizza," said the man with the deep voice. "But seeing as it's here, and I'm starving, let's open the door and take it, Vinnie."

"It could be a trap," Vinnie squeaked. "Ever think of that?"

Kyla edged over to the dresser. "Sex," she murmured. "It's me."

"Smells like pepperoni," the man with the deep voice said. "Youse know how I love pepperoni. Come on. I'll pay for it. You cover me."

"I still think you ordered it. It would be just like you, acting like we're at some slumber party."

Kyla moved the teddy bear and reached for the cat. Sex resisted, splaying all four feet out, her claws raking against the surface of the dresser. "C'mon, Sex," Kyla whispered.

"For the last time, I didn't order the pizza! It's a mistake, but I say, let's take it. There's nothin' but bean sprouts and that tutu, or tofu, or whatever ya call it, in her fridge."

The doorbell rang again and the cat tried to squeeze into the corner. Kyla got a firm grip and lifted the squirming bundle into her arms. Sex peddled with her back feet and tried to get away, but Kyla held her tight. The cat meowed.

"What was that?" Vinnie said.

Kyla hurried toward the window with Sex writhing in her arms. She grabbed the cat by the scruff of the neck, the only way she knew to make her hang limp, and swung a leg over the windowsill. Thank God for reflexology. It gave her strong fingers.

"Just the music downstairs," the other man said.

"I think it was the cat. Somethin' spooked the cat," Vinnie said. "I'm gonna check around."

Kyla grabbed for the limb and got only a slippery hold. For a moment she lost her balance, about to fall. She finally hooked her arm around the limb and managed to get one leg over it. Sex hung like a dead weight from her hand. She had to have both hands free to climb down. Vinnie was coming.

A soft voice floated up through the branches. "Drop the cat. I'll catch her."

She looked down. There was Pete, his arms stretched upward. She heard Vinnie's footsteps come closer. He would shoot them both without a thought.

4

KYLA DROPPED THE CAT and heard a muffled gasp. Sex must have landed with her claws out. Then Kyla scrambled silently down the tree. Any minute she expected Vinnie to pop his head out the window, point his gun at her and shoot.

Except he didn't. Instead she heard him holler back at Dominic, who had apparently opened the door to the pizza man. She froze against the branches, her heart pounding, and listened. She didn't want the delivery person hurt.

"Come on!" urged Pete from below her.

She motioned for him to go to the car, but he stayed at the foot of the tree. The argument between Vinnie and Dominic raged on, and at last the apartment door slammed.

"I hope you choke on it!" Vinnie yelled.

"Aw, have a slice, Vinnie."

When Kyla finally heard the pizza truck start up, she scrambled the rest of the way down the tree. Ahead of her Pete ran through the yard and out through the break in the fence. She sprinted after him, and by the time she threw open the passenger door, he'd started the engine and was guiding the car down the alley.

She hopped in and resisted the urge to slam the door. She wanted out of there, and now, but they had to be cautious. "Careful."

"Uh-huh." Pete maneuvered the car to the end of the alley, where he flicked on the headlights. Finding a break in traffic seemed to take forever. At last he swung into the street and gunned the engine.

"We did it! We did it!" Kyla bounced on the seat in her relief, then quickly scanned the area around them. "Nobody's even following us. We got the cat, Pete!" She reached over and landed a resounding kiss on his cheek. "You were fantastic."

His response came through clenched teeth. "Get her off me."

Kyla glanced over and saw that the panicked cat was rooted to Pete's thigh. In the darkness her eyes were all pupil and they flashed when she turned her head toward Kyla. Kyla scooted over and began unhooking the cat's claws from Pete's leg. She responded by trying to burrow deeper into Pete's lap.

"Take it easy, Kyla. She's—ahh!"

"Oops." Kyla grabbed the paw Sex had embedded in Pete's crotch and whisked the cat over to her lap. "Sorry."

His voice sounded strained. "Me, too."

"Uh, is there anything I can—"

"No."

In the ensuing silence Kyla stroked the cat and glanced surreptitiously at him. She noticed several red scratches on his hands and a couple of snagged threads in his coat, which was bad enough, but every time she thought about Sex's claw going into his . . . She winced and glanced down again. She couldn't help but notice that he seemed to be generously equipped in that department.

Not that his endowments, or lack of, should be of any interest to her—except when she thought of his kiss, and the moment on Jerald T. Johnson's couch. Of course the couch scene had been staged. Pete hadn't really wanted to be involved, although he *had* developed an unmistakable erection. A disturbing tension burrowed within her as she remembered the firm thrusting movement of his—

"Aren't house cats usually declawed?"

Her sensual thoughts disappeared in a wave of guilt. Pete had assumed he'd be dealing with a harmless animal when he'd told her to drop the cat down to him. "Well, sometimes they are declawed, but Trevor and I discussed it thoroughly, and we both agreed that wasn't a good idea." She took a breath. "Because if Sex ever got out, she wouldn't be able to defend herself."

"She can defend herself." He didn't sound appeased.

"I'm really sorry."

He made a noise deep in his throat that didn't sound conciliatory.

"As to the scratches, the best thing is lots of vitamins," she babbled on. "And I'll give you a foot massage when we get back to the hotel. It stimulates the immune system. Before long you'll be right as rain."

"No, thanks."

"Really, Pete. People are skeptical at first. Even Arturo Carmello didn't think I could make a difference in how he felt, but now he's—" Her monologue careened to a stop. *Now he's dead.*

The enormity of it finally hit her. She'd been so distracted by danger and her unexpected reaction to Pete that she hadn't fully focused on the murder of Arturo Carmello. Murder. A word she'd read in the newspapers and novels. An exotic word that didn't have much to do with her. Until now. If she'd given herself time to think, she might not have had the courage to rescue Sex. She stroked the cat with a trembling hand. Gradually the trembling moved over her whole body, until she was shaking uncontrollably.

She stared out through the windshield at the taillights of the cars ahead of them. Instead, she saw the red stain that had spread from the hole through Arturo's heart. She closed her eyes, yet still she saw it. Those men, who had sounded relatively normal as they argued over a pepperoni pizza, had done that. They'd given no more thought to the act than buying a candy bar. After snuffing out Arturo Carmello, they'd admired the artwork in his office, artwork he'd painstakingly collected. Now he would never see it again.

Life obviously meant nothing to them. They could have easily killed Trevor's cat just because she mewed too loudly or got hairs on their pant legs. With a little moan Kyla gathered Sex closer.

At the next stoplight, Pete put a comforting arm around her shoulders. "Don't worry." His animosity seemed to be gone. "It'll be okay."

His concern after what he'd been through made maintaining her self-control even harder. Yet, at the same time, she cherished the support of that strong arm. Pete had thrown her a lifeline and she wasn't ready to let go just yet. She cleared her throat of the emotion clogging it. "What's . . . what's your last name?"

"Beckett. Didn't I tell you before?"

"I didn't think you wanted me to know."

"I guess you're right." He drove for a while without speaking. At last he broke the silence. "Kyla, there has to be somebody you can call for help. I can understand avoiding the police for now, but isn't there someone in Chicago you can turn to?"

She began to tighten up. Despite his arm around her shoulders, he was withdrawing the lifeline, trying to get rid of her. Yet she could hardly blame him. "I moved here five months ago. I'm still getting settled and don't know many people."

"Then someone where you lived before, maybe. Your parents, or—"

"Not my parents." Yes, he definitely wanted to get rid of her. And after what he'd just risked for her sake, she had to give him that option. "Pete, maybe you should pull over and let me out." She slid from under his arm toward the passenger door, taking Sex with her. "You've done more than anyone could expect, and I'll never forget it. I'm sure I can manage by myself now."

He looked stunned. "That isn't what I meant."

"It's okay, really. I understand what a mess I've put you in, so simplify your life and let me out at the next intersection. You have plenty to worry about—your sister and brother-in-law—without me lousing up—"

"That's enough." His voice was rough-edged.

"But—"

"I said that's enough. We're going back to the hotel, cat and all. I didn't go through all this just to drop you off somewhere. How long do you think you'd last, with no money, no protection and that cat in your arms?"

In a flash she donned her protective emotional armor. "Hey, mister, I don't need your pity. If that's what—"

"It's not pity, dammit!"

"Then what is it?"

"Damned if I know! But you're coming back to the hotel with me, and you're staying there until it's safe to come out. Is that clear?"

She gazed at him in wonder.

Even he seemed surprised by the depth of his anger and the force of his command. He gave her a funny little smile and shrugged.

"I guess it's clear, Pete," she said, still amazed at his reaction.

"Good."

Her attention remained glued to him for the rest of the ride. Could it be, after all these years, that she'd found herself a hero?

VINNIE HAD COMPLAINED about the pizza, but then chomped down more than his share, claiming they had to finish it before it got cold. Then he had left Dominic to clean up the mess while he prowled around the apartment. He'd explained that he'd felt a draft.

Dominic heard the bedroom window slam and then Vinnie, looking superior, stalked into the living room. "Youse is soft, Dominic. Letting that cat out the window instead of shooting it, like I said. Now I *know* you're the one who has to take care of that girl."

"I didn't let no cat out."

"Yeah, yeah."

Dominic shrugged. "The girl's not showin' up, is she?"

"Don't you think I noticed? Don't you think I figured out we might have to start lookin' for her? Okay, here's what we do. We search this place for pictures. I want us to know her mug as good as we know our own sisters'."

Fifteen minutes later Dominic and Vinnie sat on a couple of Kyla's floor pillows and pored over the scrapbook they'd found. Vinnie ripped a picture out and held it up for closer inspection. "I keep thinkin' about that broad we seen makin' it with the guy on the couch. Did you look at her good?"

"Not good, Vinnie. That guy was on top of her, and he had that big coat on."

"Me, neither, but her hair looked a lot like this one's hair." He studied the picture in his hand. "I think we gotta go back to that office tomorrow, talk to the boss."

"But Vinnie, isn't that kinda risky? Goin' back there?"

"Oh, so now youse is worried about risky? Risky was that museum of art tour through the guy's office, your usin' the can. Now everything's changed. Now we stick our necks out, hope they don't get chopped off." He heaved himself up from the floor pillow. "Let's get outta here. She's smarter than we thought, but we're gonna get her, right, Dominic?"

Dominic gazed at the picture in Vinnie's hand. "Right, Vinnie." Vinnie blamed it all on him, but Vinnie wasn't so smart, neither. And Vinnie wouldn't always be telling him what to do. For the first time in thirty years Dominic realized that he didn't like Vinnie all that much.

TO SMUGGLE SEX through the hotel lobby and onto the elevator, Kyla borrowed Pete's coat again. "She doesn't like this," she said, closing the coat around the squirming cat.

"Just don't let her get away."

"I won't." Kyla held her arms over the bulge at her waist. "Let's go."

They marched past the doorman, through the glittering lobby and over to the bank of elevators without incident, although Kyla had to suppress a moan of pain when Sex dug her claws into Kyla's stomach. She sighed with relief when an elevator arrived.

Pete took her elbow and steered her inside. "So far, so good," he murmured.

Kyla turned as a David Niven look-alike in a dark suit entered the elevator behind them. She glanced at the man's lapel pin and groaned inwardly. He was the assistant manager of the hotel.

The man smiled and leaned against the side railing of the elevator as the doors whisked shut. "You folks enjoying your stay with us?"

Sex picked that moment to move, and Kyla clutched her stomach.

Pete stepped closer and put his arm around her. "As much as could be expected considering my wife's condition. All right, darling?"

"F-fine." Kyla closed her eyes as Sex dug in deeper.

"This has been a somewhat difficult pregnancy," Pete explained to the assistant manager. "I brought her here in hopes she'd be able to relax."

Kyla opened her eyes and smiled weakly at the man. "I probably have a future Bears star." Sex squirmed again. "He's already practicing his tackles."

The man stared at her and his pencil mustache twitched. "Uh, how far along is it?"

"Six months—" Pete began.

"Eight months—" Kyla answered at the same moment.

The assistant manager's gaze darted from one to the other.

"It's actually eight months, dear," Kyla said finally. "It's true we've *known* for six months, but the time of conception was . . . well, you remember."

"I certainly do, darling." He gave her a look that could melt Antarctica.

Kyla glanced quickly from that heated look and gave a little laugh. Good thing Pete was only play-acting or she'd be throwing herself into his arms. "Men never get these things straight," she explained to the assistant manager. Sex started climbing toward the open collar of the coat. "This baby is almost here, darling," she cooed at Pete. "I hope you're ready."

"More than ready, dearest." Pete moved around so he partially shielded Kyla from the man's view. His hand hovered between her breasts, and when Sex's ears protruded from the collar, he shoved the cat's head back down.

Sex's meow was muffled, but distinct. Kyla mimicked the sound, then made it again and nestled up against Pete. "Don't get romantic here, darling," she said, batting her eyes and keeping her voice high. "Not in front of the assistant manager of the hotel, for heaven's sake."

Pete gazed down at her, a grin on his face, his hand poised ready to repeat the maneuver. "But you're so beautiful in this condition. I long to touch you, my love." The top of Sex's head popped out again and Pete pushed it down.

Kyla timed her little squeal of feigned delight to cover the cat's meow. "Honestly, darling," she squealed.

"I can't help myself, dearest."

Kyla bit the inside of her lip to keep from laughing. On the other side of the elevator the assistant manager coughed, and shortly afterward the elevator bumped to a stop and he exited without a word to either of them.

When the doors closed and the elevator started up again, Pete's shoulders started to shake.

Kyla let out a giggle and soon was laughing so hard she couldn't keep her hold on Sex. "Oh, no," she gasped, still helpless with glee. "Here comes the baby."

"That's the ugliest kid I've ever seen," Pete said as Sex wiggled out through the coat collar.

"I can't believe we fooled that guy. How did you imagine we'd get away with pretending I was pregnant?"

Pete grinned. "It was a long shot, but fortunately for us the assistant manager isn't too bright."

"Fortunately," Kyla agreed, holding Sex against her shoulder and smiling at Pete. "Thanks a million, darling." The endearment slipped out easily. She'd meant it to be funny, a continuation of their charade. Yet it hung in the air between them with more meaning than she'd intended.

His eyes darkened a shade and his grin faded into a soft smile. *Oh, no.* More than play-acting was going on here. She should have seen it coming when he'd kissed her in the car, but the potential in that brief caress had been partly absorbed by the terror of the moment. Now the terror was gone, at least temporarily. Apparently she wasn't the only one who'd indulged in fantasies in the past few hours. From the look on Pete's face, he'd entertained his share.

The elevator stopped at their floor and still he kept his gaze on her. She swallowed and forced herself to speak. "We're here."

"Hmm? Oh." He seemed to snap out of a trance. "Let me see if the coast's clear." He held the door open and peered out into the hall.

Kyla's heart thundered in her ears. She'd asked to share this man's hotel room on an impulse, as the only way out of a crisis, but it looked as if she'd created a new predicament in the process. Fantasizing in a darkened car was a harmless game that affected no one, but if it turned out that Pete had been thinking along the same lines, the fantasy was over and reality had begun.

She didn't like it when a problem sneaked up on her like this. She viewed a mutual sexual attraction the same way she viewed a ticking bomb. She couldn't do anything about his reaction, but she had to dismantle her own feelings...or be emotionally blown to bits. As her mother had been. Surviving a relationship meant being in charge, and being in charge meant never being taken by surprise.

The look they'd exchanged *had* taken her by surprise. With luck he'd been as startled as she by the electricity arcing between them. But her experience with men had taught her that once an idea occurred to them, they were quick to follow it up with action. They'd be alone in the hotel room, where she'd be vulnerable to the whims of her body and the temptations of his. She had to plan a defense.

5

"COAST IS CLEAR." Pete glanced back at Kyla. Sex was balanced on her shoulder like an old-fashioned fur boa. The sharp-clawed cat would do a fair job of deterring Pete from acting on what kept coming to mind, but he doubted Sex would stay in Kyla's arms forever. Besides, a cat made a lousy chaperon, and Pete had a feeling he needed a chaperone for the night ahead.

As he and Kyla hurried down the hallway toward the room, he conjured up an image of Lillian to set his mind back on the proper track. He pictured explaining this zany night to Lillian and almost laughed out loud. Lillian the Cautious wouldn't understand. Besides, he wasn't well known for his daredevil antics, either. She'd argued that point when he'd announced he was flying down to help Peggy. "You're not the type, Peter," she'd said. Until that moment he'd been thinking the same thing, but something about her patronizing air had galled him into proving her wrong.

He'd never be able to tell Lillian about Kyla. At worst she'd break off the engagement, and at best she'd lecture him unmercifully about being a fool. Which he probably was. But he was having a hell of a good time being Kyla's knight in shining armor.

As he opened the door and then closed and locked it behind them, he wondered if he should consider reversing the plan and telling Kyla about Lillian. He played the conversation through in his mind. No. Any way he constructed it, an explanation seemed pompous and Victorian, as if he were informing her that he was taken. She'd done nothing that made such an explanation necessary. *Except lie under you and moan, and insist on staying in your hotel room, and talk you into rescuing a cat named Sex, and vamp with you in the elevator and call you "darling."*

"What a great place for Sex."

Pete's head came up with a snap. Surely she hadn't read his thoughts so clearly. But no, Kyla wasn't even looking at him. She'd followed her cat over to the windows that faced Lake Michigan. Sex hopped up on the windowsill and poked her nose against the cold glass.

Kyla took off the trench coat and draped it over a chair before walking toward the windows. "You like that, Sex?" She crouched and scratched the cat's ears. "Look at the lights!"

Pete swallowed. God help him, he wanted her to touch *him* with affection, speak to *him* in that sweet tone of voice.

She glanced back at him. "I didn't notice before that the sills were so low. She'll be amused for hours."

And what would amuse the people in this room for those hours? Pete wondered. Kyla stood and peeled off the extra sweater he'd loaned her. The two sweaters stuck together, and as she worked his off, the white one underneath inched up to reveal a strip of creamy skin above her jeans. The sweater was over her head, so she couldn't see how he stared longingly at that luscious glimpse of her. His lower body tightened. Damn, he'd better distract himself.

As she whipped the sweater over her head, he glanced at the cat, which prowled the window ledge. "I meant to ask you before, what happened to her tail?"

"She's a Manx. Born that way." Kyla folded his sweater and laid it over the back of a chair. Then she straightened her own sweater and fluffed her hair.

She looked wonderfully mussed, as if someone had been tussling with her on a bed, as if someone . . . there he went again, off on that dangerous track. The cat. He would make conversation about the cat. "Does she sharpen her claws on the furniture?" He pretended to care, when in reality he wouldn't have minded if the cat shredded everything if only he could . . . but he couldn't.

"I don't think she will. She has a scratching post at home, and she's been taught to use that. But we will need one piece of equipment I hadn't thought of."

"What?"

She cocked her head at him. "A litter box."

Pete looked at the cat, then at the cream-colored carpet. He had his distraction.

"Maybe there's some place around here that sells stuff like that," she suggested.

He had an immediate negative reaction to leaving her alone while he went shopping, at least so soon after they'd outrun the bad guys. Maybe he was being over-protective, but he couldn't help it. "Let's improvise something instead of going out to buy it."

"Okay." Kyla tapped her chin. "I have an idea, but you'll have to go down to the kitchen and convince someone to give you a dishpan and a large spoon. If I were you I'd slip them some money as a bribe." She paused. "I feel so helpless without my purse or checkbook. Could we make an agreement that you'll run a tab on what I owe you?"

He looked at her, knowing that would never work. To pay him back after this was over, she'd have to track him down in Minneapolis. He didn't dare mix her into his life there. But unless he agreed to her suggestion, she'd feel bound to restrain every move because of expense. "We can run a tab," he said, and was rewarded with her grateful smile. "So you want a dishpan and spoon?"

She nodded. "So you can dig in the planters."

"In the planters?" Even as he protested he found himself dreaming up ways of doing it. He was actually having a great time.

"You can—"

"I can make one trip down for the dishpan and a second for the dirt. And I'll use the coat."

Kyla beamed at him as if he were her star pupil. "Exactly how I would have handled it."

"That's a scary thought." Pete put on the coat and checked his wallet to make sure he had a twenty to bribe the kitchen help. "Don't open the door unless it's me. And you might want to turn on the news and find out whether they've found Carmello. TV's in that cabinet."

"I figured it was." She glanced at the armoire but made no move to approach it. He didn't blame her for not wanting to hear about the murder again. She looked at him and smiled. "Thanks, Pete."

"No problem." He had the impulse to kiss her on his way out, but summoned the willpower to resist it. He should never have allowed himself the luxury of that kiss in the car.

Still, as he walked out the door he carried her smile with him as if he were a knight sporting the scarf of his ladylove on his sleeve. He'd never been involved in such craziness in his life: the water tower incident paled in comparison. He'd never felt more alive.

The dishpan and spoon turned out to be easy. After learning from Kyla that there had been no news reports about Carmello, he put the second part of his plan into effect. For the dirt he took a plastic laundry bag from the closet and tucked it and the spoon in his pocket.

"If anybody questions you, tell them you're a scientist studying the effects of cigarette smoke on planter soil."

He paused at the door to gaze at her. "If I didn't feel deep in my bones that you were on the level, I'd have no trouble believing you're a con artist."

"I'm not."

"For which a whole society can thank its lucky stars. Keep the door locked." As he left he realized he didn't have to warn her about the door. She had incredible survival instincts. He wondered what kind of a life she'd had to develop instincts like that. Wondering wasn't a good sign, either. It meant he wanted to know more about her, which meant his interest was progressing beyond the sexual to the emotional. This game was becoming trickier by the minute.

On the tenth floor the assistant manager got on the elevator with him. The guy seemed to be everywhere. He smiled uncertainly at Pete. "How's your wife?"

Pete thought fast. Apparently he'd been around Kyla long enough to pick up her technique. "Actually, she's upstairs reading about primitive childbirth techniques, and she wants to try something rather bizarre to calm the baby. I don't think it will make any difference, but I'd rather humor her than have her get hysterical."

"And what technique does she want to try?" The assistant manager looked a little sick to his stomach.

"Mud packs on her stomach. She made me promise I'd get her some dirt from the planters downstairs."

A look of alarm appeared on the assistant manager's face. "From the planters? Oh, my, I don't know if we can allow—"

"When my wife gets hysterical, she gets pretty wild. I remember one time, in another hotel, she started running up and down the halls screaming about cockroaches."

"Oh, dear." The man's Adam's apple bobbed up and down. "In that case, allow me to help you collect the dirt for your mud pack. Perhaps if we take a small amount from every planter in the lobby it won't create such a problem."

"I would be most grateful. As one man to another, this has been a very trying time."

"I can imagine. Well, actually I can't imagine." He fidgeted with the knot in his tie. "Never been married, myself."

"If you ever do, I'd think twice about getting pregnant."

"Oh, I certainly will," the assistant manager said solemnly.

Thus Pete found himself following the assistant manager, who insisted on wielding the spoon, as they progressed from planter to planter.

At one point the assistant manager eyed the bag, which contained about three quarts of dirt. "Is that enough?"

Pete thought of the dishpan and shook his head. "She has a big stomach." He heard someone gasp and glanced sideways at a sequined woman who was staring at him, wide-eyed. He lifted the bag of dirt. "For my wife," he explained, and watched the look of horror creep across her heavily made-up face. He didn't know when he'd had such a ball.

When the bag was three-quarters full, Pete judged it to be enough to keep Sex happy and off the cream-colored rug for a couple of days. "That should do it," he said, holding out his hand for the spoon. "Thanks."

The assistant manager glanced at the spoon as if seeing it for the first time. "Isn't this one of ours?"

"Actually, yes. We asked room service to bring it to us so that my wife could take her Pepto. She takes a lot, and those little teaspoons weren't cutting it."

The assistant manager glanced at the spoon and back at Pete. "You have my sympathies, sir. I'll have another large spoon sent up directly."

"You are too kind." With a little bow that Pete felt was a nice touch, he took the bag of dirt and headed for the elevators.

IF PETE THOUGHT he'd had fun getting the dirt for the litter box, it was nothing compared to describing the scene to Kyla. She laughed until tears filled her eyes. "A mud pack?" she gasped, doubling over in another fit of laughter. "Pete, that was inspired."

"You should have seen that woman's face when she thought I was gathering dirt for my wife to eat." Pete loved watching Kyla laugh. She put her whole body into it.

"I would give anything to have seen that." She held her sides. "And then that business about the spoon. I—" She paused, suddenly alert.

He realized at once what she'd heard. The television had been on when he'd come back, and it had just started broadcasting the news.

"Chicago lost one of its most enigmatic citizens today," the WGN anchorwoman said. "Police are investigating the death of Arturo Carmello, who was found tonight shot to death in his Michigan Avenue office."

Pete watched as the camera showed a stretcher bringing a sheeted body out of the office building. He glanced at Kyla and noticed the rigid set of her shoulders. She'd been so free before, so happy. Dammit. Dammit to hell.

The telephone rang, and he knew it must be Peggy, but still he jumped, and so did Kyla. "My sister, I'll bet," he said, wishing he could fold Kyla in his arms and soothe away the fear in her eyes. But that wasn't a good idea, even if the phone hadn't been ringing. He crossed the room to answer it.

Peggy's voice was a whisper. "We saw the news. Jerald turned white as a ghost."

"Where is he now?"

"In the bathroom. I think he's throwing up, but he won't let me in. What should I do?"

Pete wrestled with the problem, trying to decide if his sister and nieces were in any danger. "You could take the girls and fly down to Springfield." His gaze flicked to Kyla. She looked so forlorn.

"And how would I explain that to Mom and Dad? They'd be really upset if they suspected any of this."

"Just tell them you and Jerald had a fight. It wouldn't be far wrong."

Peggy didn't respond. Finally she whispered, "I won't leave him, but I will send the girls down to Springfield. I'll say Jerald and I need some time alone to work out a few problems. I'll tell the girls the same thing. It's not as if they've never heard we have problems."

"Okay." Pete wondered if one of the reasons he'd avoided marriage so far was because he'd watched Peggy's tumultuous one and recoiled from sharing that fate. "Listen, do you want me to come over and talk to Jerald now? I'll have to sooner or later, so—"

"No!" she cut in. "Maybe we can get through this without his ever having to know what you did. He's scared. I think he'll try to get rid of those accounts if he can."

"He's said that?"

"No. He's pretending his dinner gave him food poisoning. But what difference does it make if he never tells me, as long as he gets out of it?"

Pete thought it made a big difference, but he didn't say so. "Well, holler if you need me."

"Thanks. I think he's coming out now. Talk to you later." Peggy hung up the phone.

Pete replaced the receiver and ran his hand over his face. If only he knew what to do. He was afraid of making the wrong move and lousing everything up. Maybe he'd already loused everything up.

"How is she?"

Pete was taken aback by the concern in Kyla's voice. She'd never met Peggy. Yet he shouldn't be surprised. This was the woman who'd risked her life to save a cat. "Her husband still isn't admitting anything, but he's throwing up a lot."

"How helpful."

Her disdain for Jerald was exactly what he needed to hear right now. He gazed at her, appreciating once again her strength of character. "Yeah, he's a real prince, that Jerald." He wanted to punch the guy's lights out, but it helped him let off steam by talking about him with Kyla. "At least Peggy's going to send the girls down to my parents' house in Springfield."

"But she's staying?"

"Yes. Unlike her husband, she has character."

Kyla nodded. "I think I'd like Peggy."

"I think you would, too." Pete realized with a start that Peggy would also like Kyla. Too bad they'd never meet. He glanced at the television, where other news had supplanted the story about Arturo Carmello. The digital clock on the set flashed ten-fifteen. "Maybe we should order something to eat before the kitchen closes down."

"I'm not very hungry."

Pete decided there was one constructive thing he could do. He could encourage Kyla to eat. "Think of your cat. I'll bet she's starved and too polite to say so."

That made Kyla smile. "If she were starved, we'd know about it. I'm not sure why she's not, but she'll probably want something before long. I suppose I could order fish so she could have some."

"I'll get fish, too, and save some of mine. That way we won't have to order fish again for breakfast, which might arouse some suspicions."

Her smile widened. "If mud packs and giant spoons for Pepto-Bismol don't arouse suspicions, nothing will."

"You know what I figured out? The more outrageous you are, the less people think you're putting something over on them. That guy figured nobody would make up a thing like that, so he went along with it."

"He was also dumber than dandruff."

Pete grinned, proud of himself for lightening her mood. "That, too." He walked to the desk and picked up a leather-bound menu. "Let's eat."

THE MEAL made Kyla feel a little better. Or maybe it was the company. She and Pete exchanged sister and brother stories, although Kyla edited out any episodes involving her abusive stepfather. She discovered Pete was two minutes older than his twin and that he had two loving, supportive parents whose major fault was extreme caution.

"Even two minutes makes a difference," she said. "I bet you were expected to be the responsible one."

"So were you." He pushed aside his empty plate. "Sounds as if you've been a second mother to Trevor."

She shrugged, uncomfortable with the spotlight on her. "I'm his sister. We take care of each other. You feel the same way about Peggy."

"Yeah, I do, but . . ." He studied her.

From the way he was looking at her, she knew he'd start asking more questions soon, and she didn't want to talk about her stepfather. Not tonight, after what she'd just been through. "I still haven't given you that foot massage." She got up from the small table where they'd eaten dinner. "Take off your shoes and socks while I get the hand lotion from the bathroom."

"That's okay, Kyla. The scratches on my hands don't hurt, and I—"

She paused on her way to the bathroom. "I want to do it. It's one way I can make up for all you've suffered because of me."

"To tell you the truth, I feel silly taking off my shoes and socks and having you rub my feet."

Kyla recognized that protest. Most of her male clients had voiced some version of it at first. Women didn't. They loved the idea from the moment they heard about it, but men were different creatures, especially Midwestern men. She returned to stand in front of Pete. "You think it isn't very macho to have a woman massage your feet?"

He flushed. "That's not it. I just—"

"That is it, so you might as well admit the fact. You think it's a sissy thing to do, don't you?"

He met her challenging gaze. "Yeah."

"Then take off your shirt and sweater and I'll massage your back."

He looked alarmed and excited at the same time. "Now, wait a minute. That's—"

"Suggestive? Sexual?" She launched into her favorite topic as he shifted uneasily in his chair. "No wonder you guys all end up having heart attacks. Do you realize how you've restricted yourselves? You think massage is either sissy or sexy. You lose out on comfort, caring and release of tension."

"I don't have any tension."

"Ha."

"Well, not much."

"That's what you think."

"And you're going to take care of all that by massaging my feet?"

"What have you got to lose?"

He glanced down at his black oxfords, dulled by their trip through Kyla's soggy backyard. "Maybe I'm ticklish."

"I don't tickle my clients. Are you chicken, Pete?"

"Don't go turning this into some sort of challenge."

She folded her arms. "Well, maybe it is. I challenge you to climb out of your stuffy little rut, Pete Beckett, and try something new for a change."

He laughed. "Stuffy little rut? I haven't even glimpsed the inside of a rut from the moment you charged into my brother-in-law's office. Being around you is like a vaccination against stuffy little ruts."

"Then you should be in the perfect mood for having your feet massaged."

He sighed. "Oh, what the hell." He leaned over and began untying his oxfords. "In for a penny, in for a pound."

"That's the spirit." Kyla left in search of the small complimentary bottle of hand lotion she'd spotted on the bathroom vanity. Pete was in for a surprise. If he thought like most men, he imagined that she'd rub lotion on his feet as if she were oiling a piece of furniture and then they'd be done. His feet would be smoother, the rest of him unchanged. Conservative men like Pete were a challenge and a delight, especially now that she'd glimpsed the layers of emotion hidden under his calm exterior.

Best of all, foot massage put her back in the driver's seat. For most of their time together, she'd felt at a disadvantage with Pete; the experiences they'd shared threatened to expose all her vulnerabilities. She'd been the one running from the hit men, the one concerned about her cat, the one affected by the death of Arturo Carmello, the one hiding her abusive past.

But in her reflexology work she'd learned that everyone had vulnerabilities, and often they appeared in the course of a foot massage. Maybe Pete had a right to his reluctance. She was about to get to know him better, perhaps better than he knew himself.

6

"YOU HAVE BEAUTIFUL FEET."

Pete looked uneasy. "I'll bet you say that to all the guys." He sat on the brocade sofa with Kyla cross-legged on the floor in front of him. She'd dimmed the lights and tuned in a New Age music station on the radio.

"I've embarrassed you. I'm sorry." She rubbed coconut-scented lotion between her palms and grasped his left foot gently but firmly. The instant she did, she knew she was in trouble. Her objectivity vanished, replaced with a keen awareness of how it felt to touch his bare skin. She gritted her teeth. This had never happened before, and she wouldn't allow it now. After her fine speech declaring this was *not* a sexual experience, she would not let it be one.

Unfortunately he seemed to be feeling the same thing she was. His breathing changed. He cleared his throat, shifted in his seat. "You get corporate types to do this on their lunch hour?"

"Yep." *Easy, Kyla, don't panic. You'll relax as you work.*

"Where'd this sort of thing start?"

Her heart pounded but she kept going. To back off now would be impossible to explain without getting her in deeper trouble. But she was scared. Her reaction meant she was losing control. She couldn't afford that. "Reflexology began in the Orient. Two thousand years ago, people used it to keep each other healthy."

"The magic of touch."

She wished he hadn't said that, in quite that tone of voice. She kept her eyes focused on his feet. "Yes." The energy flow between her and Pete was intense, making her fingers seem to sing against his skin, and she was reacting to it in very unprofessional ways, very dangerous ways. She studied karate to stave off physical vulnerability, but she was now being reminded that emotional vulnerability was even riskier.

"Why are you pressing that one spot?"

"First workup point."

"What's that?"

"Your heart."

"Hmm."

She'd been careless—that was all there was to it. She'd realized an attraction existed between them but hadn't respected its power. With luck it wasn't too late to regain control of the situation. She smoothed the top of his left foot, rubbing across the sprinkling of dark hair, pushing her fingers between his toes. She distinctly heard his intake of breath.

She remembered the sailboat picture in Jerald Johnson's office, the dark hair on Pete's uncovered chest. She had imagined the bodies of her clients before as she worked on their feet, but her interest had been clinical. This time she was turning herself on. Not good. Definitely not good.

The music that was supposed to soothe and relax them both was having an erotic effect. She took a long, calming breath. Perhaps she could dream up some reasonable explanation for stopping. Perhaps she could, but she wanted to keep touching him. Her fingers savored the feel of his skin. Perhaps the danger they'd been in had sensitized her. Or maybe it was the daring he'd displayed, or the way he'd made her laugh, or the gentle way he'd soothed her after they'd rescued the cat.

"This isn't so bad, Kyla."

She glanced up to find him leaning back against the sofa, his eyes half closed. God, did he look sexy. She had no trouble picturing him lying in bed, gazing at a woman in that sensuous way. Her throat went dry.

"You have strong fingers," he murmured. His words meant nothing, but his tone contained an invitation.

"Th-thank you." She could knead a person's feet in the dark, but she broke the mesmerizing eye contact with Pete and looked intently at the movement of her hands, anyway. Her face felt warm. It was probably pink, betraying her. Had her mother been shanghaied this way, by a sudden passion that left her enslaved? Kyla pushed her thumb against the base of Pete's little toe with more than her usual force.

"Hey!" He sat up, an injured expression on his face. "That hurts!"

"Sorry." Her voice was breathy. She pushed a little easier.

"That still hurts."

"Ah." She gazed into his eyes. So he was mortal. That helped.

"What do you mean, *ah*?"

"We have some tension to work out."

"Damn right we do. The tension that comes when you're torturing my feet."

She smiled. "No, that's not where it's coming from." She avoided the sensitive spot and worked her thumb down the side of his foot. "You're very tight in your shoulders and your neck. Working it out may hurt a little, but you'll feel better afterward."

"Is this one of those speeches about it being for my own good?"

"Uh-huh." Much better, she thought. They were back to bantering, and she was the one directing the operation. She could handle this, after all. She could even flirt with him a little. He wasn't so different from other men. Maybe she'd imagined her exaggerated response to him. "Are you going to chicken out?"

He lay back against the couch with a resigned sigh. "Do your damnedest, Kyla."

PETE WASN'T A FAN of pain, but he was intrigued by the reflexology concept. Okay, he was intrigued by the woman promoting it. If he ended the foot massage, she wouldn't have any more reason to touch him. He wanted her to keep touching him.

He'd rationalized it carefully. She was a woman in distress, and he'd been honor-bound to give her shelter and protection. How could Lillian fault him for that? Assuming she ever found out, which he hoped she wouldn't. But if the worst came and she learned everything, he'd have an explanation. Naturally, this professional reflexologist would want to show her gratitude to him by massaging his feet. She had accused him of putting some wimpy or sexual stigma on it, and he had finally realized that rubbing his feet would be all in the line of duty for her—nothing more.

Except the amount of pain floored him. He clenched his back teeth together as she pressed against the base of his little toe again.

"No, don't be stoic or you won't get rid of the tension. Yell at me."

His eyes flickered open. "Not a chance."

She pressed harder. "Come on, Pete."

"I can take it. I'm—yahh! Dammit, woman!" He heard the cat skitter into the bedroom. "You're making me scare the cat!"

"Never mind her. She's heard Trevor screeching when I did his feet. She'll be okay." She kept rotating her thumb. "Let loose."

He yelled again, louder this time.

"That's it. More."

She pushed against the spot and he cried out like a wounded bear.

"Get it all out. Cover me with curses."

He did. Her strong fingers tore a string of them from his throat. The pain shot through him with the swiftness of a laser with each rotation of her thumb. Strong fingers—ha! The woman would have been a star interrogator for the Inquisition. He yelled some more, and more yet, and then—ah, bliss—she stopped. Or he thought she stopped. He glanced down and she was still rubbing. The pain had disappeared.

She smiled up at him. "Rotate your right shoulder."

He complied, and almost moaned at the pleasure of effortlessly moving muscles that functioned as though oiled. "Kyla, that's fantastic."

"Told you."

"I know, but I never imagined that you could—"

"We have the other shoulder to do."

"Oh." His euphoria evaporated.

"Just don't stop yelling. That holds the toxins in."

He tried to think of a reason to back out. "People will think something weird is going on in here."

She laughed. "The assistant manager probably already has the word out that we're very strange. I doubt anyone will bother us."

He rotated his shoulder again, then tried the other one and winced.

"If you yell right from the beginning, it'll be over sooner. And doesn't it feel great to sweep that junk out of your muscles?"

"Yeah. It's almost better than sex." He wanted the words back as soon as he'd said them. At his words, her blue eyes darkened in a way that made him want to reach for her. And he had no business doing that.

The temptation was worse knowing she didn't have a boyfriend. She had no one, but he had Lillian. Methodical Lillian, who made love as if she had a manual propped on the pillow.

"Shall I do the other foot?" Kyla asked softly.

"Guess I shouldn't go around lopsided."

"Guess not."

"Go for it."

This time he followed her advice and didn't try to hold back. The shouts flew out in great cleansing bursts, and when it was over he sank against the couch in a daze. This tiny woman with knowing fingers had made him feel as if he'd been reborn. He took a deep breath and let it out.

"You're smiling." She continued to massage his feet, but now there was little pain, much pleasure.

"Yeah."

"I told you so. You must have been carrying the world on your shoulders."

Her voice mingled with the mellow synthesizer music coming from the radio. "Maybe." He liked her voice, he realized. It was pitched low for such a small person, and now it had a sexy huskiness to it.

"Your parents expected a lot from you, didn't they?"

"Guess so." He sighed again. "And I came through. Mr. Dependable. Top grades in school. Good athlete. Steady career. Sometimes I bore even myself."

She chuckled softly, the sort of intimate laughter that belonged in a bedroom.

His body reacted to the sound and the image that came with it, of Kyla in a tangle of sheets. Kyla laughing. Kyla loving some lucky guy. Loving *him* with those capable fingers, which stroked so deftly. He wasn't aware he'd groaned, but he must have, because her hands stilled and she cleared her throat.

He opened his eyes and glanced down the length of his body, where a prominent bulge had developed at his crotch. Kyla was looking at the same spot, and her cheeks turned the color of strawberry ice cream. Her gaze lifted, and they stared at each other for a long time.

He noticed the movement of her throat as she swallowed. He longed to press his lips there. Without either of them saying a word, he knew he had only to sit up and hold out his hand and she would place hers within it. That simple. "I'm engaged." He watched the light fade in her large blue eyes.

She dropped her gaze.

"I should have told you before."

"Why?" She looked up at him again, but this time her expression was closed. "It doesn't matter to me one way or the other. You've been kind enough to help me through this mess, and I appreciate it."

"But I've led you to think—"

"No, you haven't." She pushed herself up from the floor in one graceful movement. "There are all sorts of reasons why you'd react to the massage with an erection."

"Kyla!"

She waved a hand. "Come now, don't be a prude. This is scientific, not emotional. I removed some of your tension, so perhaps you felt freer to be sexual. Then again, perhaps I stimulated your groin area in such a way that you became aroused. That's never happened with my clients before, but there's always a first time. Anyway, there's nothing personal about what you—"

"The hell there isn't." He'd recovered enough to stand up. "All of what you say may be true. I don't know enough about this reflexology business to dispute it. But I'm also reacting to you, Kyla, much as I'd rather not."

"Oh?" A glint appeared in her eyes and her dimple made a brief appearance.

"Yes, and it's damned inconvenient."

The dimple flashed again. "Sorry to cause problems."

"You don't have to look so pleased with yourself, either! It's too damned appealing. In fact, don't you have any really ugly expressions you can trot out?"

She stretched her mouth with both fingers, stuck out her tongue and rolled her eyes back in their sockets.

He laughed, although laughing was dangerous, too. Giving in to any emotion was risky around this woman.

"How was that?" She grinned up at him, and he was lost. She was too great a challenge to his self-control.

He stepped closer. "I think I have to kiss you."

"You're engaged." She lifted her chin, probably in defiance, but the movement gave him the perfect angle. "And besides, you already kissed me. When we were parked in the alley."

"Doesn't count." His head angled downward. He could see a small crease in her lower lip that made him long to taste her.

"Does too count," she whispered. Her eyes drifted closed and the pink fullness of her lips parted just a fraction.

"No." He cupped her chin in one hand and used a slight pressure of his thumb to guide her mouth open a little more. He kept watching the moist opening until he couldn't see it anymore, until his lips fit over hers and their breath mingled. Then he closed his eyes and concentrated on the sensation of her full, pouting mouth against his.

She was the texture of fine satin, but warmer, more pliant. He touched his tongue to her lower lip and heard the catch in her breath. As he edged inside, over the ridge of her teeth, he realized, to his astonishment, that he was shaking. Slowly he withdrew his tongue and lifted his head to gaze at her.

Her eyes fluttered open. Those eyes, so knowing and yet so guileless. The softness had returned. She was such a paradox—tough and resourceful one minute, warm and provocative the next. "Does that count?" she murmured.

"You scare me to death."

"Ditto."

He kept his arms at his sides and settled his mouth over hers once more. This time she welcomed his tongue inside with a gentle suction that made him grow hard instantly. He explored her mouth while the pressure of wanting her grew more insistent. Resisting the urge to crush her against him took all his control. He trembled with the strain of it. But he dared not put his arms around her. Kissing her this way was insane, but he was tired of being so damned cautious, never acting on impulse.

This time she drew away. She was breathing hard. "That definitely counts."

"I'm not so sure." He leaned toward her again. "Let me—"

"No." She held a hand against his mouth. "We're not doing this any more."

He took her hand away. "Why not?"

"You know why." She withdrew her hand from his grasp and stepped back. "Your conscience would kill you. And there's always the chance you'll miscalculate and get carried away. Neither of us wants that, do we?"

His thinking had become fuzzy on that point. "Why'd you let me kiss you in the first place?"

"Because I was curious. And you're engaged, so you're a safe bet. A responsible guy like you isn't likely to cheat on his fiancée, but I don't want to push my luck."

He lifted an eyebrow. "You sound so positive that a responsible guy like me won't cheat. You've massaged my feet and now you think you know everything about me?"

"I know a lot."

"I don't think I like your implication. You're making me sound pretty damned predictable."

"You're steady, Pete. That's comforting."

"Steady and comforting? I resent that! Come here, and let me show you how discomforting I can be."

She backed up as he started toward her. "Hang on there. Don't forget your fiancée. What's her name?"

He paused. "Lillian."

"Lillian's home waiting for you. Lillian doesn't deserve this. Lillian—"

"All right!" He turned away and rubbed a hand over his face. "You've made your point." He glanced back at her. "Curiosity, huh? Is your curiosity satisfied?"

"Yes."

"Too bad." He saw a different answer in her eyes. She was battling her emotions as much as he was battling his.

"Maybe we ought to turn in for the night," she suggested softly. "I'll take the sofa."

"No."

"But—"

"Take the bedroom, Kyla. In spite of what you think of my character, I'm only human, and my self-discipline may fade in the wee small hours. Lock yourself in."

"All right." She turned without another word.

"And take the litter box. I think the cat's still in there."

"Right." She picked up the dishpan full of planter soil and walked through the bedroom door. She closed it and snapped the lock into place.

So she didn't really want him. Until she'd bolted the door, he'd held on to a scrap of hope. Of course he didn't want to be unfaithful to Lillian, but... He stalked around the room and battled his frustration. Because of her massage his body felt fluid and energized. Perhaps she was right that the massage had freed him to be sexual. Whatever the explanation, he wanted her as he'd never wanted another woman in his life. But she had doused that glorious feeling with the cold water of conscience and then settled the matter with a locked door. He could almost hate her for tantalizing him so completely and then backing away. Almost.

7

KYLA LEANED her forehead against the closed double doors of the bedroom and drew a long, steadying breath. That had been one close call. As she'd worked the tension out of his body, she'd become even more connected to him. When it was over, and she'd glanced up and noticed his arousal, her body had begun to ache in a way that terrified her. Had he not told her of his engagement, she would have made love to him.

Lord help her, she still wanted to. Her body throbbed with unsatisfied longing, and it took all the restraint she had to stay on her side of the doors. She pressed her cheek to the pristine white enamel and traced the gilt edges of the door's carved surface with her finger. She wanted to touch him that way, trace every inch of his body, make love until they forgot all the reasons why they didn't belong together.

And then what? Would she humiliate herself and beg him to stay with her forever? That would have left him with all the power and she would have been no better off than her mother.

His engagement had given her a false sense of security. She'd figured she could kiss him without risk, but that wasn't true. She'd read about women who deliberately took married men as lovers because they didn't want to make a permanent commitment. The arrange-

ment had made sense to her once, but now she knew it
would only work in the case of a man who didn't command your soul. Pete had that ability, engaged or not.
She mustn't let him any closer. She wanted him far too
much.

THE TELEPHONE woke Kyla from a nightmare of being
chased by men with huge guns. She reached for it
without thinking. "Hello?"

A short silence on the other end was followed by a
woman's hesitant voice. "I may have the wrong room.
I was trying to reach Pete Beckett."

"Oh! Velly solly. Sayonara!" Kyla banged the phone
down and lay back on the pillow with her heart
pounding. Then she heard a different sort of pounding
coming from the bedroom door.

"Kyla? Did you answer that phone?"

"I'm sorry!" she called out. "I think it was your sister."

A groan came from the other side of the door. The
phone rang again. "Let me get it out here!" he shouted
through the door.

"Right!"

Kyla tossed the covers aside and sat up. She'd slept
in her underwear and desperately wanted a shower and
clean clothes. But she also wanted to know who was on
the phone. She scurried into the bathroom, found a
hotel robe hanging on a hook, and belted it around
herself before opening the bedroom door.

Pete was sitting at the Victorian desk, his head
propped on one hand as he talked on the phone. "No,
I'm not trying to pull a fast one on you, Peggy." He

sounded tired. "If you'll just calm down I'll tell you who that was. She—"

Kyla charged across the room and pressed the disconnect button. "I'm a maid! An Oriental maid. Just came to this country. Don't know the customs."

He glanced up at her and then tried to pull her hand away from the button. "She won't buy that."

Kyla put all the strength gained through hundreds of massages into holding the button down.

He stopped wrestling with her and sighed. "Peggy knows something's going on. She started chewing out the front desk for giving her the wrong room, and they insisted they had the right room, the one where a Mr. Beckett was staying with his pregnant wife."

"Then tell her I'm a pregnant Asian call girl!"

He grimaced.

"A refugee?"

Pete shook his head. "I'm telling her the truth. Peggy won't turn you in. You have to trust people once in a while, Kyla."

"No, I don't."

"Yes, you do. You have to trust me."

She gazed into his eyes. Slowly she removed her hand from the disconnect button.

"Thank you. Peggy? Aw, hell, she hung up." He immediately redialed. "Come on, Peggy, answer. Come on, be there, Peggy." He waited a few more seconds before slowly replacing the receiver.

"Why wouldn't she answer?"

He rubbed his bristly chin and looked at her. "Probably because she's on her way over."

Kyla's breath caught. "Just like that?"

"Peggy's not like me at all, Kyla. She acts on impulse, does crazy things. Like you."

Kyla realized what Peggy would see when she arrived: Pete looking as if he'd been tossed in a cement mixer and herself draped very suspiciously in a hotel bathrobe. "What will she think when she sees us like this? With you being engaged and everything?"

"Probably nothing." His look was enigmatic. "You see, she has the same impression of me that you do. She wouldn't be able to imagine me taking you to bed when I'm still engaged to Lillian. It would be out of character. Never mind that I almost did. Never mind that even now, as you stand there in that bathrobe, I still want to."

"Oh." The desire she'd felt last night—momentarily short-circuited by the telephone call—welled up again. "We'd . . . we'd be making a terrible mistake."

"And mistakes are to be avoided at all cost, right?"

She couldn't speak. The soft tone of his voice, as well as the intense look in his eyes, drew her in. Her fingers itched to touch him again. She had only to reach out a few inches to caress the beard shadowing his cheek. One caress and they'd be lost. They both knew it. She curled her hands into fists.

Pete held her gaze. "I've lived my whole life trying to avoid making mistakes. I don't know that it's made me any happier."

A ripple of desire made her shiver.

"How did you sleep?" he asked gently.

She swallowed. "Not well."

"Kyla—" Suddenly his expression became startled and he yelped. "What the hell?" He glanced down at the purring cat in his lap. She was kneading her claws into his slacks.

Kyla took a shaky breath. "Sex."

"Not likely as long as this cat's around. Ouch! Dammit, Kyla, could you get this portable sewing machine off me without doing major damage to me or my clothes?"

Kyla cautiously lifted the cat out of Pete's lap. "She's probably hungry."

"She's probably trained by your brother to keep nasty men with impure thoughts away from his sister." He stood and brushed gray hairs from his slacks.

"Or engaged men from doing something they'd regret."

"Regret?" Pete's gaze flowed over her, lingering at her lips, her breasts, the curve of her hip. "No. It's been a long night, and I've had a lot of time to think." He looked into her eyes. "I don't believe regret would figure into it, no matter what the consequences."

She couldn't have spoken if she'd been offered a million dollars for each word.

He sighed. "Maybe...maybe you'd better get dressed, or showered, or whatever, while I feed the cat the rest of that fish from last night."

She didn't want to leave him, not quite yet. He had just lectured her about trusting people. Trust, especially in men, was a scarce commodity in her world, doled out to Trevor and most recently to poor Arturo. Could she also trust Pete, trust him enough to let him know how he affected her? Was he one of the few men she'd met who wouldn't abuse the power, once given?

Pete scrutinized her. "Go on, Kyla. Peggy will be here in twenty minutes or so, if I guessed right. If she's not here by then, we have to go looking for her. I don't think she's in danger, but you never know."

His concern for Peggy slid the final tumbler in place and the lock on Kyla's heart swung open. Yes, here was a man she could trust. But the gods had played a terrible joke on her. They'd thrown her together with someone like Pete only to have him promised to someone else.

DRESSED IN IMPORTED Italian suits, Vinnie and Dominic walked into Jerald T. Johnson's outer office. They took one look at the blond secretary behind the desk and glanced at each other.

"What can I do for you gentlemen?" she asked, swiveling her chair away from the computer keyboard.

"We'd like to see Mr. Johnson," Vinnie said.

"Do you have an appointment?"

"We figured if we was here to invest half a million, we wouldn't require no appointment."

The woman looked startled. "Just one moment. I'll see if he's free. May I have your names?"

Vinnie cleared his throat. "Manfred Bullwinkle and Rocky Brown."

She picked up the receiver on her desk phone and pressed a button. Then she murmured something into it before replacing the receiver. "You can go right in."

Vinnie adjusted his tie. "Thanks. Say, are you one of them temporary gals?"

"Excuse me?"

"You work here all the time, or just today?"

"I've been Mr. Johnson's secretary for nine years. Is that what you mean?"

"Yeah. That's what I mean. Come on, Dominic."

"Think she bleached her hair last night?" Dominic muttered as they walked toward Johnson's door.

Vinnie lowered his voice. "I think we was tricked last night."

"Rocky and Bullwinkle. Good one, Vinnie."

"You're Rocky."

"I wanna be Bullwinkle. I—" Dominic was interrupted as Johnson's door opened.

"Good morning," said a tall man with wire-rimmed glasses. He looked unnaturally pale. He thrust out his hand toward Vinnie. "I'm Jerald Johnson."

"Manfred Bullwinkle and my business partner Rocky Brown," Vinnie said, shaking Johnson's hand.

"Come in, come in." Johnson moved aside and waved them into the office.

"Wrong guy," Dominic muttered out of the corner of his mouth as they took seats in front of Johnson's desk.

"I got eyes," Vinnie shot back under his breath.

"My secretary tells me you gentlemen are interested in looking into some investment vehicles." Johnson steepled his hands. His fingers trembled slightly.

Vinnie knew fear when he saw it. For some reason Johnson was afraid of them. The guy couldn't know who they were. But fear would be useful. Vinnie glanced around the office. "Nice setup."

"Thank you. Now, are you looking for long-term investments or a quick return on—"

"You got a boat?" Vinnie's gaze parked on the picture of Johnson with a woman and another guy. He left his chair and wandered over to examine the picture more carefully.

"That . . . that's my in-laws' boat. Do you sail, Mr. Bullwinkle?"

"Nah. The only way I like water is with a couple shots of whiskey in it." He took the picture off the wall and brought it over to Dominic. He tapped the face of the man who wasn't Johnson. "This guy look familiar to you?"

Dominic squinted at the picture. "Yeah. Yeah! He's the guy that—"

"I knew this guy in high school," Vinnie said, turning to Johnson, who by now was shaking so bad he looked as if he had palsy. "Can't think of his name, but I knew him."

"My b-brother-in-law, Pete."

"Yeah, Pete. Pete . . ." Vinnie snapped his fingers. "Last name's on the tip of my tongue."

"Pete B-Beckett."

"Right!" Vinnie pointed his finger at Johnson. "Pete Beckett. What ever became of old Pete? I'd like to look him up."

"He's a CPA in Minneapolis. Mr. Bullwinkle, about your investment plans, I—"

Vinnie glanced at Dominic. "Didja remember the checkbook, Rocky?"

"What checkbook? I never knew about no checkbook."

Vinnie looked at Johnson and shrugged. "He forgot the checkbook. Guess we'll hafta see youse later."

"I, um, all right." Johnson adjusted his tie.

"I'll just borrow this picture. So's I'll recognize old Pete."

"Uh, sure. Go ahead."

"Thanks. Come on, Domin—I mean, Rocky." Vinnie jerked his head toward the door.

JERALD PUNCHED in Pete's office number, got it wrong twice before finally commanding his fingers to work efficiently. When Pete's secretary told him her boss was out of town for a few days and couldn't be reached, Jerald's stomach started to churn. Maybe the guy did know Pete from high school. Anything was possible. But those two hoods were somehow connected to Arturo Carmello's murder, as sure as he drove a black Beamer. They were sniffing around about the Aries account.

Now that Carmello was dead, maybe they were after the money. He should've given it to them, no questions asked, but he hadn't been able to think straight, not after he'd glimpsed the bulge of shoulder holsters under those imported suit jackets. They said they'd be back. Well, they wouldn't find him sitting here like some dope waiting for them.

He punched the line to his secretary. "Cancel my appointments. I'm taking the rest of the day off."

A chuckle came over the line. "Things worked out well with those two, I take it?"

"Uh, yeah. Yeah, that's it. If anyone calls I'm just . . . out."

PETE PROWLED the confines of the hotel room while he waited for Kyla to finish showering. He flicked on the television but couldn't find any news about Arturo's murder. He left the set on to drown out the sound of Kyla in the shower, Kyla moving around in the bathroom, Kyla putting on clothes—which meant she was without them for a while. He couldn't spend much time thinking about that. He'd loaned her a shirt but he had no idea what she'd wear with it. Couldn't think about that, either.

Although it seemed like hours to him, she re-emerged in less than ten minutes . . . in his shirt and her jeans. Her hair was damp and tousled. He thought of offering her his comb, except that he kind of liked the way she looked, all ruffled and fresh and . . . *available*. Damn, she was so available.

"The bathroom's all yours." She smiled. "Thanks for the shirt."

He mumbled a response and dashed for the bedroom. It was far too appealing how that oversized shirt hung to her knees. He pictured her without the jeans and the buttons of the shirt undone. God! He slammed the bedroom door behind him, grabbed some clothes from his suitcase and slammed the bathroom door, too.

Then he realized exactly what she was wearing or, rather, *not* wearing. Two damp bits of nylon and lace hung over a towel rack. Pete stared at them for a long time, even reached to touch them before he caught himself with a groan. Then he turned on the shower, full blast and cold. He'd shave later, after he'd shocked his nether regions into submission.

He was buttoning his shirt when Kyla pounded on the bedroom door.

"Peggy's here!" she called.

He grabbed his slacks and hopped out of the bathroom, putting one foot, then the other, through each pant leg. Peggy would be in a lather. No telling what would happen between her and Kyla if he didn't get out there. Kyla would stand up for herself, and Peggy would be furious at her for endangering her brother. He fastened the button and zipped the pants as he headed for the door. No time for socks and shoes. No time for combing his hair. He had to save those two women from each other.

He flung open the door and skidded into the room. Then he stopped and stared, open-mouthed. Peggy and Kyla sat on the sofa talking animatedly. The cat sat perched on Peggy's lap. Kyla was gesturing and Peggy shaking her head, her expression filled with compassion. They hadn't even noticed him. They looked like old friends.

He ambled over to the sofa. "Hi, Peg."

She glanced up. "Can you believe what Kyla has been through?"

Pete glanced at the scratches on his hands. "Guess not."

"To be caught there, when Carmello was shot . . ." Peggy shuddered and turned back to Kyla. "You were so lucky to get away. That was really using your wits. And then to go back for the cat. I can't believe you did that."

Pete turned to Kyla. "So you told her about Sex?" He was gratified to get a reaction out of Peggy. She really did take him for granted. It was nice to know she trusted him, depended on him, but enough was enough. Kyla had been resourceful, but he hadn't exactly been sitting on his thumbs during all the excitement.

Peggy glanced from Kyla to Pete. "Uh, no, she didn't say a thing about sex."

Pete motioned to the cat in her lap. "That's Sex. The cat's name is Sex."

"Oh." Peggy glanced at Kyla.

"My brother's idea. Short for Sex Kitten."

"Typical brother stuff," Peggy said.

Pete had heard quite enough. "Hey, what do you mean, typical brother stuff? Is that any way to talk to me after I risked life and limb to go through Jerald's files?"

Both women looked at him, then at each other. Slowly Peggy handed the cat to Kyla, stood and walked over to Pete. Taking his face in both hands, she gazed at him adoringly. "I think you are the best brother in the world, and I can't thank you enough for what you've done. You are better than Superman and Mel Gibson rolled into one. You—"

"Okay, okay." He took her hands away and backed up a step. He felt heat roll up from his collar, over his face. "You're overdoing it."

"No, I'm not. The truth is I'm flabbergasted that you agreed to help me in the first place. I'll bet Lillian vetoed it."

"She was worried about my career if I got caught and it turned out there was nothing going on."

"You bet she's worried about your career. She looks at you and sees dollar signs."

"Peg, you're being unfair."

"I don't think so." Peggy turned back to Kyla. "This is a woman who encourages her guy to work on Saturdays. Sundays, too, for all I know. Fun is a dirty word in her estimation."

Already feeling guilty as hell about his reaction to Kyla, Pete leaped in to defend Lillian with more force than he might have otherwise. "I think you're jealous of Lillian's ambition, Peg."

"No, I just don't like her." Peggy glanced at Kyla. "You won't like her, either."

"Now wait just a minute." Alarm zinged through him. "Kyla's opinion of Lillian has no bearing on anything. They'll never meet each other."

"Doesn't matter. I can tell Kyla wouldn't like her."

Pete's anger built as his good sense flew out the window. "You're a fine one to pass judgment on my choice of Lillian, when your husband deals with mobsters."

Peggy stilled immediately. Her voice became husky. "You're right, big brother. Absolutely right. For a minute I got so caught up in this adventure of yours and Kyla's that I forgot that Jerald got us all into this mess."

Kyla spoke up. "But if you hadn't called Pete down to help, I might be dead right now."

Pete felt as if someone had punched him in the stomach. He'd never thought of it quite that graphically, and now he knew he couldn't entertain the thought at all if he wanted to stay sane. Kyla was alive, and she'd stay that way. He'd see to it.

Peggy laid a hand on his arm. "You okay?"

"Yeah." He cleared his throat. "Yeah, I'm fine. I just—" He paused as a statement on television captured his attention. "Listen. I think they're updating the news on Carmello's murder."

Both Peggy and Kyla turned toward the screen. All three of them gasped as a composite drawing that looked a lot like Kyla filled it. He moved protectively toward Kyla. No one would find her. No one would hurt her. She stared at the screen, her face white, her fingers clutching Sex's gray fur.

"Homicide detectives are seeking this woman in connection with last night's murder of Arturo Carmello," the newscaster said. "She's a licensed reflexologist, and she may be the last person to have seen Carmello alive. Anyone with information about this woman, who goes by the name of Kyla Finnegan, should contact the Chicago Police Department."

"Goes by the name of?" Kyla wailed. "They're talking about me as if I'm some sort of criminal!"

Pete gazed at her, his stomach rolling at the gravity of her situation. "That's because you've just become a murder suspect."

8

DOMINIC GRUMBLED as he and Vinnie rode in a taxi through downtown Minneapolis. "We take a plane ride here—which youse know I hate—and the guy ain't here, which is no surprise, seein' as how he was on Johnson's couch last night, and his secretary has no way to get in touch with him. This ain't workin' out, Vinnie."

"But we found out his fiancée's name."

"She coulda been the one on the couch."

"Don't think so. That there had your cheatin' look to it. Or phony look, more like it. Stick with me and we'll get to this Pete guy, which will take us to the girl. I got a plan."

"Are we still Rocky and Bullwinkle?"

"Yeah."

"Can we switch?"

"Once you finish off that girl, you can call yourself anything you want, Dominic. Here. Have some gum."

Dominic took the gum, even if it would have been nicer if Vinnie had given it to him before the plane ride, to help his ears. But it was Juicy Fruit, the kind he liked. He chewed and thought about Vinnie not letting him be Bullwinkle. Vinnie was like that. Bossy.

A spot on Vinnie's temple that moved whenever he chewed his gum caught Dominic's attention. Dominic rolled the foil from the gum wrapper and bent it in two to look like a gun. As he pointed the wrapper at the little spot on Vinnie's temple, he popped his gum.

Vinnie jumped. "Stop clownin' around," he said, frowning at Dominic.

Dominic unrolled the wrapper and put the wad of gum into it. The flavor was gone. Vinnie shoulda given it to him on the plane ride.

"THEY THINK *I* killed Arturo Carmello?" Kyla dumped Sex from her lap and got up to shut off the television. A soap opera was on, and she didn't want the distracting noise. She had to think. A murder suspect. Her heart pounded with fear. It all made sense. The hit men used gloves, but her fingerprints had been all over everything. Even if the hit men took most of her stuff, they might have left something behind that had been traced to her. Besides, Arturo's secretary would have told the police about the appointment, and when they found him his shoes would have been off, his feet scented with vanilla oil.

Pete approached her, his expression grim. "We need to contact the police and tell them what you know. Hiding out will make you look guilty."

Kyla shuddered and massaged her arms. "No. They wouldn't believe my story."

"I'll corroborate it."

Peggy cleared her throat. "Uh, Pete, I'm not sure that's such a good—"

He whirled toward her. "Look, I don't give a damn if Jerald knows I was in that office! He can prosecute, for all I care. Tell him I forced you to give me a key. Tell him anything you want."

Peggy's dark eyes, so much like Pete's, sparkled. She glanced from Pete to Kyla and smiled.

He glared at her. "What's so damned funny?"

"Nothing."

"Okay, so it's settled," he said, turning back to Kyla. "Let's head down to the police station. Maybe you should put on your underwear."

The statement seemed to echo in the silent room. Pete gave Peggy a wary glance.

She looked unconcerned. "I didn't hear a thing."

Kyla put her hands to her hot cheeks. So he had noticed her stuff hanging in the bathroom. She thought of explaining to Peggy, but decided that would only make things worse. Better to return to the original discussion. "I'm not going to the police station, Pete."

He appeared relieved that they were back on relatively safe conversational ground. "You have to. The police think you did it. With my help you can clear yourself and give information about the real killers so they can be caught."

Kyla shook her head. She was determined, but she was no longer afraid. She could trust Pete; he wouldn't turn her in or give away her whereabouts. "Suppose they believe me? Which they may not. Suppose we give them a description of the two guys? Next step, we're on the news. Those guys are mobsters, with a whole organization behind them. They won't stop until they kill us. Do you want to take the chance that the police can protect us from that?"

"Not to mention tying Jerald in with the whole mess," Peggy added. "You could expose a lot of people by rushing into this, Pete. Me, the girls, our parents. I can see how much you care about Kyla and I know you want to keep her safe, but it's not that simple."

How much you care about Kyla. Peggy had dared to say such a thing out loud. Kyla avoided looking directly at Pete, but from the corner of her eye she saw a red stain darken his face.

He massaged the back of his neck. "Look, Peg, I don't want you to think that my concern for Kyla goes beyond what anyone would do for another person in a tight spot. When this is over, we'll part ways and get on with our own lives."

Peggy walked over and braced her hands on her brother's shoulders. She didn't have to reach very far to do it; she was a tall woman. "This is your twin sister you're talking to, remember? I'm tuned in. And let me tell you something else. Two minutes after I met Kyla I knew she was better for you than stuffy old Lillian. Lillian brings out the prig in you. Kyla brings out the man."

"Peggy, for crying out loud!"

Kyla walked to the other side of the room and gazed out the high window toward a choppy Lake Michigan churning under a layer of wintry clouds. She was having trouble bearing the weight of Peggy's approval. She wasn't sure she deserved it. If anything, Peggy should be chastising her for dragging Pete into such a dangerous situation. Instead Peggy was as good as telling Pete to dump his fiancée and take Kyla instead.

Her heart thudded a little faster. She'd abandoned any thoughts of her and Pete together once he'd announced he was engaged. What if he chose to toss that obstacle aside?

"I'll leave you two to work that out," Peggy said. "But I just wanted you to know, Pete, I think you'd be a fool to go back to boring old Lillian."

Pete made a disparaging noise low in his throat.

Once again Kyla tackled the job of steering the conversation back to a more neutral topic. "So you agree, Peggy, that we shouldn't bring in the police?"

"For now, yes."

"What about the assistant manager of the hotel?" Pete asked, turning to Kyla. "What if he watches the news and remembers seeing you in the elevator?"

Kyla groaned. She'd forgotten about the fussy little man with the mustache. "Let's hope he was too embarrassed to pay attention."

Peggy glanced from Pete to Kyla and grinned. "Too bad I don't have time to hear this story in detail. Unfortunately we need to work on the current problem. I have an idea how we can guide the police in the right direction without exposing ourselves. Kyla can give me a description of the killers and I'll phone in an anonymous tip."

Kyla glanced at her, impressed. "That's a wonderfully devious idea, Peggy."

"Thanks."

"Together you two are dangerous," Pete said.

Peggy ignored him. "Listen, Kyla, I'm sorry if I made you uncomfortable with my opinions about you and Lillian, but Pete's a little dense sometimes."

He winced. "Could we drop that subject?"

Peggy continued as if he hadn't spoken. "When you've known me longer, you'll get used to the fact that I speak my mind. And I hope we will get to know each other." She glanced back at Pete. "Mom and Dad would love her, too, you know."

Pete rolled his eyes.

"Just don't want to leave anything out, big brother."

"You never do, Peggy."

"Okay, Kyla, let's start." Peggy crossed to the sofa where she'd left her purse and took out a pad and pencil. "Give me the dope on these guys."

"I DON'T REMEMBER Peter ever mentioning a Manfred Bullwinkle," Lillian said. "You went to high school together?"

"Well, yeah, but we wasn't very close." Vinnie studied the cool blonde behind the desk. "Traveled in different crowds, if youse know what I mean." He'd left Dominic down in the lobby of the office building, as he'd done at Beckett's office. Looked less suspicious that way.

"I think I understand what you mean, Mr. Bullwinkle." Her long, delicate nose wrinkled faintly, as if she smelled something bad but didn't want anyone to notice she had. "So if you're not here to renew an old friendship with Peter, why are you here?"

"I heard through the grapevine you and him are engaged."

"That's correct."

"Well, then maybe I'm here more as *your* friend."

She straightened in her leather chair. "I beg your pardon?"

"I bumped into Pete in Chicago yesterday, and he was with this cute little brunette. They looked real friendly."

Her eyes narrowed. "I expect that was his sister, Peggy, and I resent your insinuation. Get out of my office." Her chair squeaked as she stood.

"Peggy?" Vinnie held his ground and remained seated. "That isn't the name I heard when he introduced us. Think it was Kyla. Kyla Finnegan. Cute little thing, about five feet tall or so. You know her?"

"You're mistaken, Mr. Bullwinkle. And if you don't leave this minute, I'm calling security."

Vinnie decided he'd planted enough of a hook. He got up. "I didn't mean to cause no trouble, lady. Just thought a classy woman like you would appreciate knowing when her guy is foolin' around."

"Out! Now! I imagine you thought you'd get some monetary reward out of me or something. I can't think why else you'd come here and fabricate such a story."

Vinnie backed toward the door. "It's up to you, but if it was me, I'd give the guy a call, ask him a few questions. Better yet, hop a plane down there. If he's not doing nothin', he'll be glad to see you. If he is . . ." Vinnie shrugged.

"Goodbye, Mr. Bullwinkle!"

Vinnie almost giggled on the way down in the elevator.

On the main floor Dominic hopped up from the marble bench he'd been sitting on. "What happened?"

"I got her to thinkin', all right. All we hafta do is watch her. I'll bet she'll lead us to her boyfriend in no time flat."

KYLA PROVIDED Pete's sister with all the details she could recall about the hit men, and Peggy immediately left to find a pay phone and call the police. Afterward she planned to drop in on her husband to see how he was holding up.

Once Peggy had left, a tense silence settled over the room.

"I like your sister," Kyla said at last.

"She likes you." Pete stood about ten feet from her, his expression unreadable.

"I—I want you to know that I have no intention of coming between you and your fiancée."

"In order for that to happen, I'd have to allow it, wouldn't I?"

"I suppose." Kyla focused her attention on the cream-colored carpet that spanned between them. As they stood there, the distance seemed to stretch like a piece of vanilla taffy. "Her name is Lillian?"

"Lillian Hepplewaite."

"Mmm."

"She's a CPA, too."

"Mmm." Kyla figured as much. "I, uh, that is, what does she—"

"Blond, tall, thin."

"Beautiful," Kyla guessed, her hopes dying away. Lillian Hepplewaite was probably everything Kyla was not, and that was obviously the kind of woman Pete preferred, despite what his sister might want for him.

"She's beautiful."

"Mmm." Kyla kept her expression blank through sheer willpower. She knew from massaging his feet that he took his responsibilities very seriously. Maybe Peggy's attack on his fiancée had made him even more determined to believe he'd chosen correctly. Earlier this morning he had seemed ready to have a last fling before he settled down with Lillian forever. She hoped she wouldn't become desperate enough to go for that.

"We haven't eaten breakfast," he said carefully. "Are you hungry?"

Kyla didn't think she could touch a bite. She wondered how she'd be able to stay in the same room with Pete much longer with her hopeless attraction growing stronger every minute. One of them needed to get out of there, and with her picture plastered all over the news it couldn't be her. "You know what I'd love?"

His eyes flickered and his body tensed. "What, Kyla?" he replied softly.

She closed her eyes. She wished he wouldn't talk to her that way, as though caressing her with his voice. She took a calming breath and opened her eyes. "Some of that fabulous streusel cake from one of the bakeries around here. The kind with the cream filling. I've become addicted to it."

"Streusel cake?"

"Yes. I'll bet there's a bakery nearby. I'm pretty sure I've seen one on Michigan Avenue. You could ask someone downstairs and blame it on the whims of your pregnant wife."

At Kyla's last words, a thoughtful look appeared on his face and he gazed at her until she grew uncomfortable under his scrutiny. She was about to take back the request and think up another errand for him when he seemed to snap out of his daze.

"I'll get my shoes and coat." He went into the bedroom.

The minutes dragged until he left the suite. When he was finally gone, Kyla sagged with relief. Any longer in his presence and she might have done something really stupid. It didn't say much for her self-esteem that she was considering a one-night stand with Pete. Okay, maybe a two-night stand. The extra night didn't make the idea any less sleazy. Unfortunately it still sounded pretty damned exciting.

Kyla decided to use the time while he was gone to dry her underwear with the hair dryer. Having it hanging in the bathroom when he went in there this morning had only contributed to the sensual tension, and she might as well do her part to reduce it. Sex was asleep on the window ledge. She'd settled in quite nicely, Kyla thought. In fact, she'd probably become so spoiled with swordfish and salmon, she'd expect the same treatment when this was over.

When this was over. Her time with Pete would end in two days, when Trevor got back to town. On the one hand, Kyla didn't know how she'd make it through the next two days; on the other, she wanted these two days to last forever.

She didn't realize the telephone was ringing until she turned the dryer off. She raced for the bedroom phone. It could be either Pete or Peggy, and either one of them could be in trouble. She grabbed the receiver and spoke breathlessly into it. "Hello?"

There was a hesitation. Then a female voice she didn't recognize said, "Is Peter Beckett there, please?"

Kyla went numb. Unless Pete had given this number to his secretary, the woman on the other end of the line was Lillian.

THE CONCIERGE had directed Pete to a little German bakery about a mile from the hotel. He walked, figuring that maneuvering the car through traffic and finding a parking space would take as long as covering the distance on foot. Besides, the cool breeze off Lake Michigan was exactly what he needed. What the hell was he going to do about Kyla? She'd pegged him exactly right. A guy like him didn't cheat on his fiancée. But then a guy like him seldom found himself in these circumstances.

To make matters worse, his sister was practically throwing him into Kyla's arms. Peggy wouldn't advocate dishonesty. She'd expect him to tell Lillian everything, afterward, of course, when his fate was sealed with Kyla.

Pete preferred things more orderly. First he'd tell Lillian the engagement was off—God, was he seriously thinking this way?—and then he'd take Kyla to bed. Except that Kyla was driving him insane with longing.

He was surprised at the things he longed for, too. Such as when she'd mentioned he could blame this streusel cake search on his pregnant wife. She'd been standing there in his oversize shirt, which could have been hiding a pregnant belly. He'd wanted it to be true. He'd never pictured Lillian pregnant with his child. He'd never imagined Lillian as a mother. She kept no pets and had never shown the smallest nurturing instincts. Yet he wanted children, didn't he?

Pete's trench coat lapel flapped in the wind. He remembered Kyla smuggling Sex under it and the gentle way she talked to the cat. She'd be great with kids, fun-loving and spontaneous when they were in a playful mood, comforting when they were upset, firm when they needed guidance.

But Lillian... Lillian would color-coordinate their wardrobe, hire a decorator for the nursery and enroll them in prestigious kiddie schools. She'd love them, in her way, but it would be a distant sort of affection. *Sort of the way she acted with him.*

And there it was. Next to Kyla's emotional intensity, Lillian's measured responses seemed pale and unfulfilling. With a sigh, he accepted the inevitable. Painful though it might be, he had to break his engagement with Lillian. The only unanswered question was when he'd do it.

He glanced up and realized he'd passed the bakery. He backtracked at a brisk pace and entered the shop. Surrounded by warmth and the smell of bread baking, he found the exact streusel cake Kyla had requested. He wished she could have been there to pick it out herself. She would have loved the place.

He hurried out the door with the box balanced in his arms to prevent the pastry from being crushed. Bringing this gift to Kyla filled him with more joy than he'd experienced in a long time. He suspected she'd sent him out of the room to diffuse the emotions building between them, but he also figured that she honestly loved streusel cake. What a treat to please someone such as Kyla, who had a large capacity for enjoyment! Being around Lillian, who was lukewarm about everything, Pete hadn't realized how much he'd missed the opportunity.

Missed opportunities . . . His pace slowed as he considered their precarious situation. Men with guns were after them. What if the men showed up? What guarantees were there that he and Kyla would make it through alive, that he would have the chance to break off with Lillian, then satisfy his longing for Kyla? To be blunt, what if he died not knowing the joy of making love to Kyla Finnegan?

Pete glanced up the street. A block farther on was a drugstore.

After making his purchase, he quickened his stride. Then, several yards from the hotel he saw it—a white patrol car, Chicago Police lettered in blue on the side. It crouched menacingly in the circular drive of the hotel. He broke into a run, the streusel cake bouncing inside the box and his coat flapping behind him. Dammit, had they traced her so quickly? He should never have left her alone. If he'd been there to answer the door, he could have made some excuse, hidden her somewhere. Dammit!

He shouldered past the doorman and raced for the elevators. One was available, and he elbowed two people aside to claim a place in it. They frowned and clucked their tongues; he didn't give a damn. God, the elevator was so slow! On the way up he took his key out of his pocket so he'd be ready. If the police were in there, he'd . . . he'd what?

For one thing, he'd make them lay off her until he called his lawyer. He doubted Kyla had one. Then, if there were only two cops, he'd find a way to distract them so she could run out, take the fire stairs to the underground garage. The rental car had gas. He'd toss her the keys. He'd hold the police off until she escaped.

But she wouldn't go without that damn cat. Hell!

Pete's heart pounded frantically as the numbers blinked upward to his floor. Pete Beckett, CPA, was standing in an elevator plotting how to outwit the police. This was more than infatuation he was feeling. This was more than lust. This was— The elevator stopped at his floor and he dashed through the doors before they opened completely.

The room door was closed. He slid the key in and opened it. Calm was the byword. They had to take him for what he appeared, a mild-mannered businessman. They mustn't suspect that in the past eighteen hours he'd developed the instincts of a criminal.

Once inside the door he heard thumping noises in the bedroom. Then he heard Kyla cry out. He dropped the streusel cake and abandoned calm. If she was trying to fight them off, he was here to help. He careened through the doors to find Kyla looking at him in surprise. She was alone.

"What's wrong?" She hurried over to him. "You look like you've seen a ghost."

"I heard a fight going on!" He glanced around, still not convinced that two men in dark blue uniforms wouldn't jump out any minute. "There's a squad car downstairs! I thought—"

"The police are in the building?" She paled and stepped back, a hand to her throat.

"I thought they were here in the room."

Her pupils widened and she shook her head.

Relief flooded through him. "Then I'm not too late. Listen, if they come up here, you'll hide, okay? I'll handle it. You're small. We can fit you in somewhere. A closet or something."

"But they'll search."

"They have to get a search warrant for that. I'll threaten to sue the hotel or something. Don't worry. We'll handle it."

"Should I leave?"

The response within him was so primitive that he almost grabbed her up in his arms right then and there. "Definitely not," he said, his voice almost a growl.

"We should hide the cat, too, in case they know I have a cat."

"Right. We'll hide the cat. We'll—" He stopped as he remembered the pell-mell way he'd raced into the room. He'd left the door open. Edging back toward the living room, he asked casually, "Is Sex in here with you somewhere?"

Kyla followed him out of the bedroom. "Last time I looked she was asleep on the window ledge." She glanced at the empty ledge and the open door. "You left the door open!"

"I thought you were in trouble." He reached out and pushed it closed. "Maybe she ran under the bed."

Kyla's voice was low and tense. "Help me look."

He shucked his coat, tossed it on the sofa, and started to search.

They combed the suite. No cat.

Finally Kyla stood in the middle of the living room, looking more woebegone than Pete had ever seen her. He felt like a bungling fool. She swallowed and tried to look brave. "Well, Pete, I think she's escaped."

9

PETE COULDN'T STAND watching Kyla struggle for composure. That damned cat meant so much to her. And hadn't he just been thinking that this same caring quality was one of the things he loved about this woman?

Loved?

No, that was impossible. You didn't fall in love in eighteen hours, especially when you'd recently professed to be in love with someone else. Anyway, he'd figure that out later. Right now he had to get the cat back. "Okay, here's what we do. You stay here and keep checking. Maybe we missed someplace. I'll look in the hall. She's probably still on this floor."

Kyla's eyes widened. "Oh, my God. Do you think she would go on the elevator?"

"I don't think she can reach the buttons," Pete said, hoping to make Kyla smile. She did, faintly. "Okay, I'll go now," he continued. "Remember we're still not sure what the deal is with the police."

"I know." She was obviously trying to control her fear.

Pete tried to speak as calmly as possible. "As long as I stay on this floor, I'll see any cops who show up. But don't answer the door. Keep the security bolt on, and they won't be able to get in. If they start demanding to come in, I'll hear the noise, even if I'm down the hall."

She nodded. "You'd better go."

"Right." He glanced at the box he'd dropped on the floor. "That's your streusel. May be a little the worse for wear."

"It doesn't matter. But thanks for getting it."

Pete thought of how he'd imagined her enjoying the pastry, how she would smile as she opened the box and saw exactly what she'd wanted inside. Dammit, things should be different. He wanted to joke with her, take a carefree walk by the lake, share a box of popcorn at the movies. Somehow, sometime, he'd make it all possible.

He opened the door and glanced back. "Don't worry. I'll get the cat." He carried her answering smile of encouragement with him as he stepped into the hall in search of Sex.

He didn't fully appreciate the problem until he found himself on his hands and knees, poking around behind a maid's laundry cart. "Sex," he called softly. "Come here, Sex."

"Is there something I can help you with?" A frowning woman in a gray-and-white uniform approached the cart and peered down at him.

Pete scrambled to his feet. "We, uh, ran short on towels."

"Uh-*huh*."

He noticed the pager clipped to her waistband and wondered if she'd report a weirdo on the floor. He thought fast. "I came to get more towels, and I could have sworn I saw a cockroach run under the cart."

"And you were trying to coax it out with sweet talk about sex? Strange bug control, mister." Her hand moved closer to the pager.

"Look, I have a problem here."

"I can see that."

Pete fished in his hip pocket for his wallet.

The maid backed away and unhooked the pager. "Look, mister, this isn't that kind of hotel. I don't care how much you're willing to pay me, I'm not risking a steady job for some kinky game."

"No, wait. You don't understand. I'm looking for a cat."

She backed away another step. "I don't want to hear about your twisted sexual preferences."

"No, no. Let me explain. My...wife has a cat named Sex, short for Sex Kitten."

"*She's* into animals?"

Pete's control snapped. "Now stop that! We're not weird. We have a pet, an ordinary pet, and we smuggled her into the hotel. I accidentally left the door open just now and she got away. If you'll help me look for her, I'll pay you twenty dollars."

She shook her head. "I'm not looking for no cat for some weirdo couple. This has already been one hell of a day. Assistant manager of the hotel charged with embezzling, and now some damn business with a cat."

"The assistant manager? The guy with the little pencil mustache?"

"That's him. Real proper type. Never could have figured he'd be like that." She looked Pete over. "But in my job I see all kinds, if you get my drift."

Pete started putting things together, and the world looked a little brighter. "I thought I saw a police car downstairs a while ago. Was it here because of the assistant manager?"

"That's right. Although I expect we could get another one here mighty quick if we needed one." She regarded him with a steady gaze.

Pete could have kissed her. The police hadn't been here because of Kyla, after all. And chances were the assistant manager had been too busy this morning with his own problems to watch the news and identify Kyla as the woman the police were looking for. "I can't believe cat smuggling is worth calling the cops."

"That all depends."

Pete took his cue and handed her the twenty, which she tucked into her uniform pocket without a word.

"Thanks." He turned and walked away, still wondering if she'd use the pager when he was out of sight. He would have to take that chance. He had a job to do. Besides, his luck was changing. He could feel it.

Once around the corner, he began calling softly for Sex again. He looked behind each heavy floor ashtray. The hotel's logo was stamped in the smooth sand filling the tops. It occurred to him that the sand could be another source of litter box filler. God, he was becoming depraved.

"Sex. Here, Sex," he called, prowling the hall carefully so as not to startle her and make her run again. He crooned more seductively, as he imagined Kyla might. "Here, Sex, baby."

A man and woman rounded the corner. From the alarmed look on their faces he figured they'd heard him calling for Sex. He shrugged and began snapping his fingers in rhythm. "New song," he said. "Can't get it out of my mind."

When they continued to stare at him, he began to sing as he headed down the hall. He threw in a dance step for good measure. "Sex, baby. Oo-oo, sex, baby." He turned the corner and leaned against a wall. For a moment he allowed himself to hate Trevor Finnegan for picking such a dopey name for his cat. That damned animal had better not have jumped into the elevator. The idea gave him cold chills.

And then he saw her, prancing down the hall toward him, not cowering or hiding as he'd imagined, but strolling regally, her little stub of a tail up in the air. She acted as if she owned the hotel. She saw him and paused.

"Well, hello there, fur ball," he murmured in a sweet voice, inching toward her. "Remember that swordfish you had for breakfast, you little monster? Come back with me and I'll order you a nice bowl of cyanide for lunch. Would you like that?" Slowly he closed the gap while she gazed at him. For the first time he noticed she had blue eyes. In the depths of those eyes, he could swear he saw laughter.

"Listen, flea bag. This has gone on long enough. You've made me look like a pervert and an idiot, and I'm not taking it anymore. Is that clear?" In the split second that she bolted, he dived and grabbed two handfuls of thick fur. She yowled and he cursed as his knees and elbows hit the carpet. But he got her. Hissing, she tried to squirm away, but he held on fast and managed to avoid her claws.

Wheels squeaked to a stop beside him. "I see you got the cat."

He glanced sideways at the maid's cart parked beside his prone body. "Yes, ma'am."

"For another twenty I'll vacuum up this hair you've strewn all over the hall."

Pete hunched himself to his feet while keeping his grip on the cat. "I'd appreciate that, but I can't let go of this feline to get my wallet."

"Hold her by the scruff of the neck. She'll think you're her mother and hang still."

"Her mother. Great." But Pete tried it. "I'll be damned. Like carrying a bag of marbles." He managed to extract his wallet and fished out a twenty with his teeth while Sex hung from his other hand, her body curved like a gourd. Replacing his wallet, he handed the money to the maid.

"For a man who's supposed to own a cat, you sure don't know anything about them."

"It's my wife's cat."

"Then why isn't she out here looking?"

"She's, um, pregnant. Very pregnant." He sketched a huge belly in the air.

The maid looked skeptical.

"Any day now. Any minute. In fact, I'd better get back there, just in case." He hurried away, conscious of the maid's calculating gaze following him until he turned the corner. He was glad she couldn't see which room he was headed for. The woman had the soul of a blackmailer, and he was running low on cash. Forty bucks for this cat.

Hell, forty bucks was nothing. He'd risked his life for her last night. He held the dangling animal up and looked her in the eye. "You'd better be worth it." Then he thought of how Kyla would react to the return of her cat, and he knew anything was worth seeing those wonderful dimples flash for him alone.

KYLA PACED THE ROOM, unable to stay still. Pete had to find Sex. He just had to. After all they'd risked the night before to rescue the cat, losing her now would be unbearable.

She picked up the box of streusel cake and laid it on the coffee table next to the crystal bowl of carnations. A glance inside revealed that the pastry was broken into several sections. She put the lid back on and didn't look at the streusel cake again. The sight of its cracked topping made her want to cry.

She'd been having that urge far too often recently. Crying was a luxury she hadn't allowed herself in years. She'd stayed tough and kept her wits about her, never truly depending on anyone. Then yesterday she'd had no choice. She still had no choice, and the act of depending on Pete was cracking her shell of independence as surely as the drop to the carpet had cracked the streusel cake.

It was a scary feeling after all these years. Yet when she looked into Pete's eyes, she believed in him, believed he was a trustworthy man. She suspected she could let her guard down completely with a man like Pete, let him know exactly how she felt without sacrificing herself in the process. There was only one problem: he was engaged.

She glanced at his trench coat flung across the sofa and decided to hang it up for him while she waited. The coat smelled like Pete, woodsy and familiar. Already she knew the scent of him. She held the inside of the collar to her nose and sniffed. Then she rubbed the nylon lining against her cheek. Something rattled in the pocket.

Had he bought a surprise and forgotten to tell her in all the confusion? Feeling like a child at Christmas, she reached into the pocket and felt a small cardboard box. Maybe he'd found some special tea to go with the streusel cake. Curious about his selection, she pulled the box out. Then she blinked. The familiar label of a condom manufacturer seemed to glow as if written in neon.

Kyla stared at the box as her initial reaction of shock transformed into a curl of anticipation, a thrumming of excitement. Wait a minute. She should be scandalized. What did he think, that she'd just hop into bed with a man who was engaged to someone else?

Except she wasn't scandalized. They'd been struggling with their attraction to each other since the moment they'd met. Their remaining time together would further challenge the limits of their self-control. Did he see this step as inevitable, despite his engagement? To be honest, didn't she?

Kyla took the coat and the box into the bedroom. She hung the coat in the closet, as she'd planned, and put the box in a drawer of one of the nightstands with a trembling hand. She'd wondered before if she was desperate enough to sleep with Pete knowing they would have no tomorrows together. As she stared at the rumpled bed, she began to think she was.

But first she'd have to tell him about Lillian's call. Just as soon as he got back, she'd tell him. If only she hadn't answered, but she'd been so certain it was Pete or his sister. Of course, even if Lillian found out about Kyla being in the room, so far Pete didn't have anything to feel guilty about. Not really.

Not yet.

Finally she heard Pete call her name as he rapped on the door. She raced toward it and fumbled in her eagerness to undo the latch. Pete stood on the other side holding a very cowed Sex by the scruff of the neck. Happiness flooded through her. "You did it!"

"I did it." He shoved the cat forward.

Kyla took Sex into her arms and buried her face in the soft fur. Her relief and gratitude, coupled with her knowledge of what was in the nightstand drawer, created a heady brew. Sex squirmed a little. "You're a naughty kitty," she murmured, waiting for her rush of emotion to pass. When she finally looked up, Pete had closed the door and was watching her snuggle the cat. "You deserve a plaque or something," Kyla said. "That's twice you've saved her."

"I think she owes me a couple of her lives."

"I owe you a lot, too, Pete."

He didn't deny it, just kept looking at her with an intensity that sped up her heartbeat.

Would he ask her straight out to make love with him, or would he lead up to it somehow? Nervously she grabbed at the first topic she could think of. "Any sign of the police?"

"Hmm? Oh." He seemed to shake off his preoccupation. "Good news about that. The police weren't here about you at all. They just arrested the assistant manager for embezzling."

Kyla stood there, taking it all in. The police weren't after her. Her cat was back. There were condoms in the nightstand drawer. She realized she needed to make a response. "Embezzling?" Sex mewed and wriggled some more. Kyla reluctantly set her down. She needed something to do with her hands. "The same assistant manager from the elevator?"

"Yep. Better yet, with all his problems this morning, I doubt if he's had time to watch the news."

The more he reduced her level of worry, the more she thought about making love to him. "How in the world did you find that out?"

"I've been bribing maids." He glanced down as Sex wove in between his legs and butted her head against his shin.

"Pete, this must be costing you a fortune. I swear I'll pay you back."

He gazed at her. "With another foot rub?"

So this would be the lead-in. They both knew what had nearly happened the last time. She swallowed. Now was the moment to tell him about the phone call and remind him of his responsibilities. "Pete, there's—"

Sex meowed.

"I need to tell you about—"

Sex meowed again, more insistently.

Pete glanced down as Sex meowed a third time. He sighed. "I guess we'd better feed this cat."

"Maybe so." A short reprieve. She would tell him in a minute, but how she hated to. By answering the phone, she'd taken away Pete's chance to keep her presence a secret from Lillian. Kyla had put him in an awkward position once again, and she didn't think he'd thank her for it. Maybe that would decide the issue of their lovemaking.

He crossed to the telephone and punched in the number for room service. "Would you like something?"

You. "Just my streusel cake would be fine."

"Coffee?"

"Um, coffee would be nice." She wanted to touch him, to put her arms around him and never let go. But it wasn't her place to do that. As soon as he ordered the food she'd tell him about the phone call. She crouched and rubbed Sex's forehead until Pete hung up the phone. Then she stood. "Listen, there's something—"

"Before we talk about anything else, I have a question." He came toward her.

Her heart started pounding again. "What?"

"What the hell were you doing when I came back with the streusel cake?"

She frowned, confused. "Doing?"

"When I opened the door I heard thumps and would swear that you cried out."

"Oh!" She flushed. "That's why you dropped the box and left the door open?"

"I thought the police had you and you were fighting them off."

"I was practicing my karate."

He gazed at her. "Karate."

"I'm a brown belt."

He lifted his eyebrows.

"I'm sorry, Pete." She rushed to explain. "I never thought how it might sound to someone walking in, and I forgot I hadn't mentioned it to you, and under the circumstances I thought maybe I should practice my— "

He reached up and touched a finger to her lips. "Don't apologize. Hell, I'm delighted you're a brown belt in karate, if it helps keep you safe." His finger traced the outline of her cheek.

The slow curve he drew along her face made the hair on the nape of her neck stand on end. "I should have told you, though."

"When?" His hand drifted back to his side, but he continued to gaze at her. "We haven't had much time to find out about each other."

How easily she could come to love this man. She sighed. "I think . . . maybe we shouldn't try."

"Maybe we can't help it."

Kyla wanted to stay transfixed by his eyes. If she didn't move, he might kiss her. Then he might take her in his arms, which she wanted more than anything in the world. But she had to tell him about Lillian. "Pete, while you were gone. I'm . . . I'm pretty sure your fiancée called." As the light slowly faded in his eyes, she longed to erase what she'd said.

His mouth tightened. "I guess you answered the phone, then."

"I'm afraid so." Misery drifted over her like fog. "I thought it must be you or Peggy. I never imagined it could be Lillian."

He turned and walked over to the window where Sex was grooming herself on the ledge. "What did you tell her?"

"Nothing. I just said hello, and she asked for you. Then I knew who she was, somehow. I couldn't think of a good line to use, to throw her off, so I just hung up."

He looked back at her and gave her a sad smile. "You, the champion of quick comebacks?"

"I . . . everything went out of my head." She couldn't tell him the visceral reaction she'd had at the sound of his lover's voice. Because certainly they were lovers. In this day and age engaged couples usually were. She hadn't been able to think of a dodge this time because she'd wanted to rage and cry and throw the phone across the room.

He closed his eyes.

"Pete, it doesn't have to be a problem." Her heart ached for him, for herself. "You can explain why I'm here, and that I was expecting you to call about something and when I heard a woman I just hung up. I know it seems suspicious, but after all, we haven't really done anything wrong." *But I want to. I want to make love to you, to do all the things Lillian may be imagining we've done. And you must want it, too, or you wouldn't have made that special purchase.*

Still he didn't speak.

She wondered if he was remembering the box in his trench coat pocket. She hurried on, trying to help him through this. "I'll talk to Lillian, if that would help. I'll tell her the truth, that you were dragged into this mess and you have no interest in me other than helping a fellow human being."

He gazed at her. "You can't tell her that."

"Why not?"

"Because it would be a lie."

The look in his eyes took her breath away. "Pete—"

"I decided on the way to the bakery that my engagement to Lillian is over."

She pressed a hand to her chest, as if that would quiet her racing heart. She'd thought he'd say that he'd decided on the way to the bakery that they would make love. That she could handle. But this—ending his engagement because of her—was a whole different thing.

She was so frightened of the commitment his words implied she could barely speak. She'd prepared herself for illicit lovemaking. This was something far more powerful. "But we've known each other for less than a day."

"I've told myself that. It doesn't matter. I've known Lillian for two years, and yet I've never felt for her anything close to what I feel for you." He didn't approach her, as if he had to say these things and gauge her reaction first.

This is for real, Kyla. This is the big time. You have a chance at something special, if you have the courage to take it. He's tossing aside the engagement, which you thought was in your way. But your own fears are in the way now, aren't they? She began to shake.

"You're not saying anything. Is that because this is a one-sided feeling on my part? If so, you'd better tell me now."

Her voice came out in a whisper. "There's so much you don't know."

His shoulders straightened, as if he were bracing himself for a blow. "You're already married."

"No, nothing like that."

Relief flashed in his eyes. Then they twinkled. "You prefer women."

She almost laughed, except she was so scared. "No, Pete. It's just that I've never..." She searched for the right words.

"You're a virgin?"

This time she did laugh, although her laughter carried a trace of hysteria. "In a way. Call me a mental virgin."

"You're not making sense. It's a simple question, Kyla. How do you feel about me?"

"It's not a simple question!" She hugged herself, trying to stop the shaking. "I don't want to end up like my mother. Mostly, when I look at you, I don't think I would, but then I thought you were engaged, so I felt safe, sort of. And now you're ready to end the engagement, and you want to know how I feel. I'm scared, Pete!"

He took a step closer. "What happened to your mother?" he asked softly.

Oh, God. Tears. Tears pushing so hard nothing would hold them back.

"Kyla—" He crossed the room with swift strides and gathered her close.

At first she tried to push him away, but he wouldn't let her. The sobs rose up, and she tried to swallow them back, but as he drew her insistently against his solid chest, as he murmured things she couldn't even understand, as she felt his compassion wrap around her as surely as the strength of his arms, she let go.

And it hurt. Every sob erupted with such force that it shook her whole body. Hot tears scalded her eyes and her head pounded with the weight of sorrow coursing out of her. She couldn't stop any of it. There seemed to be no end.

But at last, there was an end. Pete stroked her back as she hiccuped and snuffled against the wet wool of his sweater. She rested her cheek there and listened to the beat of his heart. It was the most important sound in the world.

A knock sounded at the door. "Room service," called a voice.

Pete continued to stroke her back as if he hadn't heard a thing.

"The . . . salmon," she choked out.

"We'll get it later."

"But we ordered it."

"So what?" He brushed a damp bit of hair back from her cheek and leaned down to kiss her forehead. The waiter called and knocked again. "People change their minds."

She snuggled closer. She didn't want to move even a quarter inch away from him. She wondered if he'd ask any more questions, but he didn't. He just kept holding her, stroking her back, pressing his lips against her forehead. The waiter knocked one last time, and then there was silence.

Kyla sighed. "I guess he went away."

"Mmm."

She sniffed again. "I haven't broken down like that in a while."

"So I gathered."

"Guess I'm not such a tough little cookie, after all."

"Oh, yes, you are."

She took a deep breath. "My stepfather beat my mother, Pete. All the time. Sometimes he beat us."

His arms tightened around her and his heartbeat quickened, but he didn't say anything.

"That's why I learned karate. Trevor, too, when he was old enough to practice. But the thing I couldn't understand, was why she stayed, why she still stays. Whenever I ask her, and I mostly don't anymore, she says it's because she loves him." Kyla shuddered and buried her face against Pete's chest.

He caressed her hair and remained quiet for a moment. "You know that's not love," he said at last.

She rested her cheek against his chest again. "I try to tell myself that, but when I began having these feelings for you, and I realized what power they could have over me, I thought 'Is this why she stays? Is this what I didn't understand?'"

He groaned and tucked his finger under her chin. Gently he raised her damp face so he could look into her eyes. "Love and pain don't have to go together, Kyla."

She was enraptured by the expression on his face. Yesterday she'd thought him handsome. Now she thought him beautiful. His eyes radiated a caring that enveloped her and brought a shaky smile to her lips. "I never wanted to test it before."

Slowly she reached up and touched the tiny lines fanning out from the corner of his eye. Then she trailed her finger down the slight crease in his cheek, evidence of a million smiles. She'd never noticed before how perfectly shaped his lips were, how tempting the little groove between his mouth and nose. She traced it with the tip of her finger.

He gazed down at her. "Would you like to test it now?"

10

KYLA FELT as if she were standing at the edge of a precipice. If she leaped, there was a chance she would fall. There was also a chance she would fly.

"Yes," she said.

He swept her up into his arms so fast she laughed. He paused and glanced down at her. "Is this funny?"

"No. This is wonderful."

He leaned down and gave her a lingering kiss. "Mmm. Yes, it is." Then he started toward the bedroom again.

"Don't you need your trench coat?"

He stopped and looked at her as if she'd gone crazy. "What, you want to relive that moment on Johnson's couch?"

Kyla grinned and shook her head.

"Then why would I need my—" His frown cleared and he looked a little sheepish. Then he glanced back to where his coat had been draped over a chair.

"I hung it up for you."

He smiled down at her. "And you snooped."

"You schemed."

"No," he said softly. "I hoped."

The amount of vulnerability packed into that simple statement melted her fears. "Oh, Pete, make love to me."

"For as long as you'll have me." He held her gaze as he carried her through the double doors. When he laid her on the bed, Sex meowed in the other room. He brushed his lips against hers. "I'm closing the doors," he murmured.

"Okay."

The moment he moved away and she no longer touched his reassuring warmth, the cold doubts returned. What was she doing, baring her heart and soul to someone this way? She'd been too open with him. He'd take advantage of that. Men usually did. This was the biggest mistake of her life. The stakes were too high this time. She wanted him too much.

As he returned, passion etched on his face, she quailed inside. He was formidable, dangerous, unknown. Panicked, she sat up.

He paused. "What's wrong, Kyla?"

"I—I shouldn't have been so hasty. Maybe, under the circumstances, we shouldn't . . ."

He waited for more explanation. When none came, he said softly, "What circumstances, exactly?"

"Well, you know, the pressure of being together. We're not thinking clearly."

"You'll have to do better than that."

"All right." Her words came in a rush. "I never cry, and especially not in front of people. But I did today. I've let down my guard for some reason. I don't seem to be myself, and that scares me, really scares me, Pete."

He started to say something, shook his head and started again. "You have to know I won't hurt you."

"How can I know it? You can't make a promise like that."

He stared at her for several seconds. "No, I suppose not. That was probably a stupid thing to say." He lifted his gaze to the ceiling. "Everything I think of sounds stupid to say." He paused, took a breath, and looked at her again. "But at least believe this, Kyla. I would never hurt you the way your stepfather has hurt your mother. Never."

She desperately yearned to believe, yearned to trust him enough to take the most frightening step of all—fall in love. She watched as he struggled with his emotions, and her heart ached. He wanted her. No doubt about that. But with that wanting, would he try to dominate her, too?

His hands clenched. "We don't have to make love."

She could tell the words had been difficult for him to say, but he'd said them. She couldn't deny his self-control. "The trouble is, I do want to make love," she said softly. "And it says a lot about you that you noticed I was scared. Another man might have plowed ahead." She hesitated. "Maybe everything would have worked out if you had."

"No. It wouldn't have worked out. I don't want you to be scared." He didn't say anything for a while, just studied her, his expression intense. He finally spoke, but hesitantly, as if afraid to hope for too much. "Maybe, if . . . if you're in charge, if you're in control. . . ." His voice trailed off.

Something eased inside of her. "Yes," she murmured, knowing immediately he was right. "Yes."

His chest heaved. "Then command me, Kyla," he said gently.

Her heart swelled with excitement. She would be in charge of this beautiful man. She would direct his loving, his caresses.

"I'll do whatever you—"

"Stay...there for a moment." In a flash she knew how she wanted it to be. Part of her control would come from undressing now, before he touched her. She slowly began unbuttoning the shirt he'd loaned her to wear. She'd never gotten around to putting her underwear back on, and now she was glad.

He stood very still while she unfastened each button. As the last one slipped free, he let out a long sigh. She parted the shirt's lapels and let the oversize shirt slide from her shoulders. He didn't speak. He didn't have to. Her nipples puckered under the bold heat of his gaze. The room was so quiet she could hear the faint honk of a car from the street far below.

Pete swallowed. His voice shook. "God help me. How I want you, Kyla."

She wanted him, too. Yet she wouldn't tell him that just yet. Even his restraint must have limits. She unfastened her jeans, lifted her hips, and in one smooth motion removed them. He made a noise low in his throat but stayed where he was.

"Now you," she murmured. "First your shoes and socks."

He reached down and stripped them off.

Then she pointed to his sweater. "And do it slow."

His hands trembled a little, but he drew the sweater over his head deliberately, without rushing. Then he unbuttoned his shirt while he kept his gaze locked with hers.

"Take your time," she murmured. He had given her a precious gift in letting her direct him, and she wanted to record every moment of this first undressing, this first removal of barriers that screened his body from the rest of the world. Her heart pounded and the beat reverberated through her.

He pulled his shirt from the waistband of his slacks and fumbled with the last few buttons. Glimpses of his body told her he was more magnificent than she could have imagined from the picture of him by the sailboat. He drew back the shirt and removed it in a motion that thrust his chest boldly forward. She mentally caressed the flair of his collarbone and the bunched power of his pectoral muscles. The flat disks of his ocher-colored nipples nestled beneath a light tracery of hair.

He dropped the shirt to the floor and quickly reached for his belt buckle.

"Too fast." She put a trembling hand to her throat.

His movements slowed, but his breathing quickened. His chest gleamed, covered by a fine mist of sweat. He unbuckled the belt and drew it through the loops in one long, restrained movement.

She swallowed, nearly robbed of speech by the sensuous gesture. "Very good."

His voice, burned by his passion, rasped in the stillness. "I'm here to please you, Kyla."

She had to remember to take a breath as he dropped the belt to the floor and gradually unfastened his slacks. His fingers shook, but he eased the zipper down with delicious leisure. Beneath the opening his erection thrust against the white cotton of his briefs. A pulsing rhythm began at the juncture of her thighs as she watched with anticipation.

The slacks crumpled to the floor and he stepped out of them.

Desire thickened her vocal chords. "Everything," she managed.

He hooked his thumbs in the elastic and wrenched the briefs down. Kyla's eyes widened as she saw how lavishly he was endowed. He kicked the briefs away and stood before her, a Grecian god in full arousal. "Any more instructions?"

"Come here," she whispered. "Come here and kiss me."

He stepped forward, to the edge of the bed. "Kiss you . . . where?"

"You can . . . start with my mouth."

He put one knee on the bed and leaned forward enough to settle his lips on hers. The scent of his skin and the tingle of his warm breath on her face sent rivers of heat through her. Trembling and a little dizzy, she stretched out on the rumpled bed.

He followed her down, his tongue dancing over the curve of her lips.

"Touch me," she breathed against his mouth. "Make it go slow."

Resting on one elbow, he reached with his other hand and feathered a caress behind her ear. With excruciating slowness he traced down a fraction, where he toyed with the small gold hoop she wore in her earlobe. Her breasts ached for his hands, his mouth, yet she didn't guide him there. He would arrive in his own time. And she, driven crazy with waiting, would forget to be afraid.

As he stretched beside her, the heavy press of his erection against her thigh teased her with the promise of what would be, and an aching hunger such as she'd never known began deep within her. As he kissed her, he outlined the curve of her jaw with his finger, and his forearm brushed as if by accident against her nipple. She moaned, her response muffled by his mouth over hers.

He lifted his head and gazed down at her. Rich passion deepened the brown of his eyes. He smiled. Watching her face, he drew his finger down between her breasts where moisture was gathering. Then he brushed his finger across her lower lip before leaning down to kiss her again, a short kiss, just enough to make her pant for more. Still watching her, he traced the swelling outline of her breast. Then he drew a smaller concentric circle, and one smaller than that, as if creating a bull's-eye.

As he neared the pulsing tip, she closed her eyes and begged, in a hoarse whisper, for what she wanted. Cupping her breast in one strong hand, he leaned down and ran his tongue around the aureole. She groaned, and at last he closed his mouth over her.

"Yes!" Shamelessly she arched her back and tunneled her fingers through his hair as his rhythmic suction drove her closer to the edge of mindlessness. She'd never felt this way, never wanted a man to completely possess her.

With an almost animal growl of satisfaction he released her and took her other breast. Yet now she wanted more than to be caressed. She needed to caress in return. She reached for the smooth length of his shaft and wrapped her fingers firmly around it. He gasped and lifted his head to look into her eyes.

She made a cylinder of her fingers and glided them down over the solid warmth of him until the heel of her hand encountered the springy mat of hair beneath. He closed his eyes.

"Look at me," she whispered, and stroked back up.

He opened his eyes, and they were filled with such naked passion that they stirred an answering demand in her. Slowly she guided his hand down between her thighs.

"Ah, Kyla. We're getting close now." He pressed intimately, probing through the damp heat and soft folds until he touched the wellspring of her response. "There?"

She had little breath left to answer. "You don't even have to ask."

"No."

His touch, soft yet constant, set her on fire. "That's enough," she gasped. "Don't—I need us to—"

"So do I." His hand stilled. "But I didn't want to leave you behind."

She shook her head. He glanced toward the closet and started to leave the bed. She caught his arm. "I put them in the drawer."

His gaze swung back to her and his eyes glittered with desire. "Seems I wasn't the only one anticipating this moment."

"I think you knew that."

"No, but I love knowing it now." He kissed her deeply before rolling away from her. She heard the slide of the drawer, the crackle of the cellophane and the snap of the latex. Then he turned back to her. She reached for him.

He grinned and gathered her close. "That's the Kyla I was looking for. The no-holds-barred, all-out Kyla."

"She's here."

"In all her glory." He moved over her and braced his arms on either side of her head. His smile faded as he looked into her eyes. "In all her glory," he whispered.

Her heart swelled with the joy of being cherished.

"Tell me what you want, Kyla."

"You." She cupped his buttocks. Guided by the pressure of her hands, he entered her gently, sweetly, never taking his gaze from hers. He glided forward, his presence within her more gift than invasion. As her emptiness slowly filled with him, she moaned in pleasure.

"Good?" he murmured.

"Wonderful. Oh, Pete . . ."

He drew back just as carefully and eased forward again. Perspiration dotted his forehead, and she realized he was restraining himself with great effort. He didn't want to hurt her, but oh, this ecstasy was a long way from hurt. She braced her hands against his shoulders and rose to meet him. She wanted all the sensation she could get. Instinctively she rotated her hips, bringing her into more intimate contact.

He gasped. "Oh, Kyla, when you do that, I want to—"

"Then do it."

With a groan he relaxed his arms and moved closer until his chest rubbed her taut nipples as he moved. He increased the tempo.

She matched him, stroke for stroke. "Yes!" she cried, her fingers digging into his shoulders. "Pete, that's good, so good."

"Ah, talk to me," he whispered urgently in her ear. "Talk to me, Kyla."

"There. Right there." She lifted her hips to increase the friction. "Oh, Pete, that's ... yes ... more, please, more ..." As the tension built she couldn't think in words, so she praised him with little cries of delight and moans of pleasure. He surged against her, his body damp, his moans mingling with hers. She had never allowed a man to sense her total surrender, but she allowed it now. She abandoned herself to the sensations.

The first spasm shook her. No time to turn back.

"Kyla!" His rhythm spoke of a frenzy beyond his control.

"Now," she whispered, and was swept away by a climax that erupted with a force that blocked out the world.

With a cry of exultation he joined her, and as her own orgasm receded, she felt the pulsing of his completion. And he was laughing, laughing with such joy that she caught his mood of celebration and began laughing, too.

He hugged her tight and laughed some more. "There is such *life* in you." He raised himself up and looked into her face. He'd smiled at her before, but not like this, not as if his cares had disappeared, as if he anticipated something wonderful would happen very soon. For a long, sparkling moment they absorbed the wonder of so much happiness.

At last he spoke. "Peggy's right. You bring out the man in me, and the boy, and the daredevil. I like who I am when I'm with you, Kyla."

She reached up and traced his happy smile. "So do I."

He gazed at her with a tenderness that made her want to weep with the sweetness of it. "You know," he said lazily, "you give a damned good foot rub, but this has it all beat."

She smiled. "Foot massage has its place. Not everyone has access to this sort of relaxation technique."

"And speaking of that, I claim sole access to this particular relaxation technique with you."

Her heartbeat accelerated. "What . . . what are you saying?"

"I'm saying that I—" He paused and his smile faded. Sorrow tinged his eyes. "But I can't say that yet, can I?"

"Maybe not, Pete." The shimmery excitement began to disappear.

"I have some . . . matters to take care of before I say anything, Kyla. What happened here was . . . You see, I began to realize life is so uncertain that—"

"Hush. I understand." She caressed his cheeks with both hands, wanted to rub the sudden tension from his jaw. "I know you have to talk to Lillian."

He sighed. "And I don't think I should do it over the telephone. That means postponing the plans I want to make with you until I can go back and face her with the news."

She could see the prospect of telling Lillian was eating him up. Better to get it over with. "Why couldn't you go now?" she said softly.

"And leave you alone? No way."

"Pete, I'll be fine. I can have room service leave food outside the door, and I'll keep the security bolt on all the time."

"I don't like the idea."

"Pete, there's another thing. Lillian already suspects you have a woman in your room. The sooner you explain the situation, the better. She could be stewing about that phone call right now. It's not fair to her, especially considering your plan to break the engagement."

Pete leaned his forehead against hers. "You're right. God, you're right."

"I'll be fine, Pete. Go. Then we can get on with ... whatever we want."

He lifted his head. "You know what I want. Kyla, I've never felt like this with a woman. I thought I was basically an emotionless man."

That made her smile again. "Hardly."

"If I schedule a flight out, I'm booking another one back here two hours later. I can say what I have to say to Lillian in that time. And I'll be back before you miss me."

"No chance."

He groaned. "I love hearing that, but it's going to make it damned hard to leave."

VINNIE STARTED the engine of the rental car. "Taxi pulling up, Dominic. Whatcha wanna bet Lillian comes out of that apartment building and gets in it?"

"So what?" Dominic hunched down in the seat and blew on his hands.

"So we follow her."

"She could be goin' anywheres."

"Not with a suitcase, she ain't."

"She's got one?" Dominic sat up straighter and peered across the street. "Damned if she don't."

Vinnie looked triumphant. "And youse thought it was some coincidence that she left work early. Now watch this, cousin. I'll bet we follow her right to the airport."

"I still don't think we'll be able to get tickets on her plane, Vinnie."

"A dame like her gets to the airport in plenty of time. We'll get on. Even if it's full, somebody's gonna want to sell their seats for a profit."

"What if she recognizes us?"

"Keep your hat brim down and don't say nothin' and stay away from her. Besides, what if she does recognize us? We could be flyin' back to Chicago, couldn't we? It's a free country."

"This trip ain't free. It's costin' a lot of money," Dominic grumbled. "Pretty soon we'll use up all that we got for doin' the job in the first place."

"You think I like that? I'll give youse your choice. Spend the money or go to the pen. Take your choice."

"I don't like them choices."

"It's too late to complain about it, Dominic. Maybe next time you'll think before you decide to take a leak in a dead man's office."

11

PETE HUNG UP the bedside phone and turned back to Kyla. The white sheet swathed the lower half of her body, leaving her breasts uncovered as she lounged on the bed. He guessed that she knew the effect that pose would have on him, and he reveled in her sensuality. Remembering the texture of her nipples against his tongue was all it took for him to want her again.

Her knowing smile told him she understood exactly how he was reacting. She touched his hand. "First we need to talk. What did the airline say?"

He had to think for a minute as to what she meant. Oh, yes. Lillian. "First available flight to Minneapolis is in three hours. The good news is there's a return trip about two hours after that. I won't be gone long."

"I keep telling you I'll be fine."

"You, lady, are mighty fine." He allowed himself the luxury of reaching over and stroking one creamy breast. Her blue eyes grew smoky, like the humid haze of a Midwestern summer day. He was glad the first available flight wouldn't take off for three hours. He had at least an hour and a half before he had to leave for the airport. He rubbed his thumb across her nipple and watched it spring to pert attention. Her eyes drifted shut and her head lolled back. Watching her reaction, he grew hard instantly.

Then her eyes opened and she lifted her head. "Listen," she whispered.

He tensed. A muffled sound like a popcorn popper came from the other side of the door. What now? And what could he do about it sitting here stark naked? Passion forgotten, he shifted his hand away from Kyla's breast and surveyed the room for a potential weapon.

Kyla laughed. "It's only Sex."

His anxiety changed to irritation. "What the hell is she doing now?"

"Digging her claws into the carpet to get our attention."

"Great." He stood and walked over to the double doors. When he opened them Sex gazed up at him with wide blue eyes. "Why can't you just scratch on the door, like normal animals?"

"Dogs do that," Kyla said. "Not cats. She's either lonesome or hungry."

Pete hoped she was hungry. He wanted more uninterrupted time with Kyla. He remembered the meal they'd ordered, which had probably gone back to the kitchen when they hadn't answered the door. He could order another one. He turned back to Kyla. "Maybe we should get her something to eat." He remembered that he and Kyla had eaten less than the cat had in the past few hours. "And something for us, too."

"I suppose we should."

He grinned at her. "Have to keep up our strength." Then he glanced down at the gray cat. "Come on, fuzz face. We're ordering room service again." He walked into the sitting room for the menu. He couldn't remember ever strolling around a hotel suite without clothes on, and it felt great. "Same order as last time?" he called back to Kyla.

"Sure."

He picked up the phone and remained standing while he talked to room service. Sitting might have invited a cat to jump in his lap. With Sex's willingness to use her claws on his anatomy, she could ruin his plans for the next hour and a half.

Giving the order must have sidetracked his brain from lovemaking to food, because his stomach grumbled. As he hung up the phone, he noticed the streusel cake box. He crossed the room, picked up the box, and carried it into the bedroom with Sex trotting at his heels. "Let's start with this," he said, putting the box on the bed beside her.

"Great idea." As Kyla sat up, Sex hopped up on the bed and began sniffing the box. "That's not for you." Kyla picked up the cat, cradled her in her arms and scratched behind her ears.

Pete couldn't take his gaze away from the erotic picture she made with the fluffy cat nestled against her breasts. "Someday..." he murmured, then stopped, astonished at how uninhibited he'd become and how quickly fantasies developed when he was with Kyla.

"Someday what?" She glanced up and the blue of her eyes matched the blue of the cat's eyes.

He was bewitched. "Someday I'm going to make love to you while you're wrapped in fur and nothing else."

Her lips parted slightly and her breasts quivered as her breathing quickened. "But not real fur. I don't believe in killing animals for their pelts."

"No, not real fur." He thought of Lillian's mink. He'd always hated the coat and had never considered asking her to put it on while she was naked. She wouldn't have done it, anyway. He'd never imagined himself the kind of man who would be aroused by the picture of fur gliding over the smooth skin of a woman. He savored the image now. And he was getting other hedonistic ideas, too.

He leaned down and took the cat from Kyla's arms. "I'd better put her in the other room until the rest of the food arrives," he said, inventing an excuse. "We don't want cat hairs in the streusel cake." His body was already reacting to his fantasies.

Kyla assessed his condition and her dimples flashed as she relinquished Sex. "I do believe you've forgotten about the streusel cake."

"Not exactly."

She lifted an eyebrow.

"Be right back." He was grateful that the cat allowed herself to be put out with little more than a soft mew of protest. He was about to return to the bed and pursue his fantasies when a knock came at the hall door.

Kyla chuckled. "Room service again."

"Those people have the lousiest sense of timing I've ever seen."

Sex meowed at the door and started her claw-digging routine again.

Muttering an oath, Pete found his pants and pulled them on, easing the fabric gently over his erection.

"You'd better hide Sex in the bedroom while you answer the door," Kyla said.

He zipped his pants and sighed. "I'm tired of hiding Sex."

She laughed at that, and he grinned. Her laughter was so precious to him, it made up for his uncomfortable state. "Just a warning. I'm giving the cat some fish so we can be undisturbed for a while," he said over his shoulder as he headed out the double doors of the bedroom. He scooped up Sex and dumped her on Kyla's side of the doors. The cat stayed meekly where he'd put her. "Good, Sex," he crooned before closing the doors firmly behind him. Kyla's laughter followed him like a breeze through wind chimes.

He signed for the food, and after the bellhop left he let Sex out of the bedroom, dished some salmon onto a saucer and put it on the floor. Then he returned to the bedroom, closed the doors behind him and turned to find Kyla sitting in the middle of the bed eating streusel cake with her fingers.

She glanced up. A glob of white filling clung to her upper lip and she removed it, catlike, with a flick of her tongue. Desire pounded through him and he decided that with Kyla, every movement was sensual and suggestive.

He shucked his pants with a sigh of relief and eased down next to her on the bed. "Taste good?"

"Mmm. Have some." She reached for another piece.

He put a restraining hand on her arm. "Wait."

She glanced up.

Fantasy time. "Let me feed it to you."

Pink tinged her cheeks. She ran her tongue over her lips and her eyes grew dark and mysterious. "You'd like that?"

"I'd love that."

"Then do it."

A surge of need left him feeling a little dizzy. Trembling, he broke off a piece of the streusel cake and slowly brought it up to her lips. She nibbled it from his hand, her white teeth nipping at the crust and her tongue curling over the creamy filling in the center. He groaned.

She looked at him from beneath her lashes, then returned to her task. When the main bulk of the piece was gone, she slid her tongue over his palm. His groin began to ache with a ferocity that made him draw in a sharp breath. Then she licked between his fingers, where some of the filling had oozed down. Finally she took his little finger in her mouth and sucked gently. He thought he might come apart from the pressure building within him.

She released his finger and gazed into his eyes. Her voice was husky and rich with passion. "Now I'll feed some to you." She scooped another chunk from the box and held it close to his mouth. Nothing had ever tasted like this. The sweet topping crunched under his teeth and the creamy filling squashed deliciously onto his tongue. He ate hungrily, making more of a mess than she had, and powdered sugar sprinkled from her hand onto her breasts. He let it fall.

He finished the piece she'd held for him and grasped her hand so he could work his tongue over her palm and between the crevices of her fingers, as she'd done with him. She sighed. He drew circles on her palm with his tongue. Then he licked the inside of her wrist and traced the faint blue veins under her soft skin. She moaned and swayed gently.

"You have sugar all over you," he murmured.

She glanced downward, her eyes dreamy. "So do you."

He followed the direction of her gaze. She was right. He'd sprinkled her breasts, but also himself, including the throbbing shaft that boldly announced his ultimate intentions.

"Something should be done," she whispered. In one graceful gesture she eased down and began lavishing the same treatment on him that he'd planned for her.

"Ah, Kyla," he groaned as each flick of her tongue brought him closer to paradise. He leaned back on his elbows, closed his eyes and wondered if this much pleasure could kill a man. Even if it could, he didn't think he had the will to make her stop.

She closed her mouth over the sensitive tip and he gasped as new waves of ecstasy washed over him. With Kyla he was a conduit of sensations; she'd awakened his whole body. As she vainly ministered to him, pleasure zinged outward to his fingers, his toes, his lips. Even his ears tingled.

And she wasn't going to stop. Submerged in a vortex of pleasure, he dimly realized she would continue until he was sated. He couldn't let her do that. Couldn't. In that final moment of release, he wanted to be buried deep within her. "Stop," he murmured. "Stop, Kyla."

She lifted her head. The wild abandon in her eyes almost put him over the top.

He drew her up to him and kissed her long and hard. She tasted so sweet, a heady combination of passion and pastry. He never wanted to give up the taste of those lips. Continuing to kiss her, he rolled to his back, bringing her with him. The bedside table drawer was still open, and he fumbled with one hand for the package.

She raised her head and smiled down at him. "Let me."

His heart thundered in anticipation as he handed her the condom. She wasn't an expert, but she was so earnest about the task that he didn't dare take over. What's more, her gentle fumbling worked him into such a state that he had to stare at the ceiling until he got some control back.

"There."

He let out a long breath. "You are one hell of a woman."

"A woman who wants you." Holding his gaze, she lowered herself onto him in one slow, deliberate stroke.

He clenched his teeth against the explosion that threatened to end this carnival of pleasure. Then he gazed up at her. The view was spectacular. The underside of her breasts beckoned to him and he cupped a hand under each. She leaned into his touch, bracing her hands on either side of his head, and he drew her down until he could taste her sweet skin. Bits of sugar remained, and he licked them away. All the while, she moved her hips in a gentle circle that drove him wild.

He couldn't last much longer; he knew that. Her movements changed to a back-and-forth rhythm that would take care of him in no time. He stopped kissing her breasts and instead watched her expression as she moved. She was beautiful caught in the throes of passion this way—her eyes half closed, her lips full and pouting, her skin glowing as if suffused with an inner light. He wanted her to climb the heights with him, but he sensed she was concentrating all her efforts on him.

Reaching to where they were joined, he pressed his thumb against the sweet spot that propelled her own lusty response. Her eyes fluttered open and her pupils grew wide. "Yes," he whispered. "You, too, Kyla."

Her breathing changed, and he knew he'd found the way to bring her with him. He applied more pressure, rubbing gently until her quick breaths turned to gasps and finally cries of delight. He drank in the sounds of her, the sounds he loved, as he coaxed her closer, closer.... And she was there, driving against him with such frenzy that he couldn't hold his own climax a moment longer. Calling her name, he clutched her hips and rode the wave to its glorious peak. At the final moment, he knew he'd never been higher.

KYLA DIDN'T WANT Pete to leave, not even for three or four hours, but she had to let him go. Only minutes remained of their time together, and without her consciously willing it to happen, her automatic defensive shield was slipping into place between them. As the moment of separation drew near, her dreams of happily ever after receded. What if, after seeing Lillian again, he reconsidered? What if Kyla became a passionate but forgettable incident in his life?

They'd showered and then eaten most of the food on the room service tray. It had tasted like tree bark to Kyla, but she'd forced it down because she didn't know what else to do. They'd watched the news, but nothing startling had turned up on the Carmello murder. Apparently Peggy's anonymous tip hadn't yielded any results yet. Pete tried Peggy's house and got no answer, so Kyla promised to try again several times while he was gone. Now they lay fully dressed and facing each other on the bed.

"I don't want to leave you," he murmured, stroking her hair.

Her emotions in full retreat, she steeled herself against responding to his touch. She couldn't afford it now. "It won't be for long."

"I wish I could take you with me."

"It wouldn't work. You have to talk to her alone."

"Maybe I should wait until this other business is wrapped up and those thugs are caught."

Kyla wasn't worried about the hit men anymore. That danger had faded in the face of losing Pete to Lillian. And she might as well find out tonight whether that would happen. "I'll be perfectly safe. You have to talk to Lillian right away. This is the best plan. Let's go with it." She sounded like a robot, but she couldn't help herself. She knew the sort of reassurances he wanted, but she was incapable of giving them to him.

He frowned and cupped her cheek in one hand. "I can feel you closing me out. Don't do that, Kyla."

She remained silent.

He stroked her cheek and combed her hair back behind her ear. "You're afraid I'll go back to her, aren't you?"

She wished she could declare passionately that she thought nothing of the kind, but she was so scared. When she was scared, she hid. He meant everything to her. She'd vowed never to become this vulnerable, yet it had happened. If he didn't come back to her, she might not survive the emotional wreck.

"Oh, Kyla." He pulled her close and cradled her head against his chest. She forced herself to remain limp in his arms. Lifting her chin, he looked deep into her eyes. "Please believe in me. I will be back, and we will talk about our future. I'm not going to hurt you."

She didn't trust herself to speak.

"Goddamn it." He kissed her hard, thrusting his tongue forcefully into her mouth.

It took every bit of restraint she had to lie quietly in his arms. He slid his hand beneath the shirt she wore, and although she couldn't control a quiver as he touched her breasts, she willed herself to remain passive.

At last he sighed and gazed down at her, his expression desolate. "You've gone away somewhere."

"It's better this way."

He shook his head. "Kyla, we could comfort each other. We could—"

"Just go, Pete."

His smile was so sad it ripped at her heart. "And I was hoping you'd beg me to stay." He removed his hand and adjusted the shirt over her breasts. Lowering his head, he kissed her again, more gently this time. "I'll be back," he whispered. He left the bed and went to the closet for his coat. "Keep the door locked and bolted." Then he was gone.

Kyla lay on the bed, her eyes dry. She'd dulled her emotions so completely that she couldn't even cry. If she stayed this closed off from her feelings, she'd be prepared if he came back and told her he was going to marry Lillian, after all. She had to be prepared for that. It was the only sensible way to face an uncertain future.

Sex hopped on the bed. Putting each paw down carefully, as if walking a tightrope, she made her way across the mattress. She sniffed Kyla's face, and her damp nose butted against Kyla's.

"Go away, Sex." Kyla felt her defenses begin to crumble.

The cat started methodically washing Kyla's cheek, licking away the salty tears that began to flow. Her tongue felt like a damp loofah sponge, eroding Kyla's control.

A sob rose in Kyla's throat and she put her arm around the cat and pulled her gently away from her task. "Don't do that," she whispered in a choked voice. "I can't take it."

Sex stared at her with unblinking eyes. Then slowly she turned around and hopped off the bed.

"There." Kyla took several deep breaths. "That's better." She glanced at the digital alarm clock on the bedside table. Only three hours and twenty minutes to go. She watched the numerals roll by. Maybe she could stay on the bed until Pete came back. That might be the safest thing.

The phone rang, shattering the stillness. Kyla's heart pounded. It couldn't be Pete. He was on his way to the airport with little time to spare. He might even be at the airport by now if traffic had been light. But the caller could be Lillian. Kyla imagined picking up the phone and telling Lillian that Pete was on his way to break the engagement. She could tell Lillian about the passionate afternoon she and Pete had spent together. What woman would stay engaged to a man after hearing a thing like that? Yet Kyla didn't pick up the receiver.

Eventually the phone stopped ringing. A few minutes later it started again.

"Hang on, Lillian," Kyla muttered. "You'll have your shot at getting him back. You'll have it very soon." As she listened to the shrill summons, Kyla remembered she'd promised to call Peggy. Pete needed to know that Peggy was all right. Kyla needed to know, too. She liked Peggy.

Her body felt like lead, but she dragged herself from the bed and went into the living room where Pete had scribbled Peggy's number on a hotel pad. When the ringing stopped for the second time, Kyla picked up the receiver of the desk phone and punched in Peggy's number.

Peggy answered immediately. She sounded excited. "Hello?"

"It's Kyla, Peggy. Are you all—"

"Thank God! I've just tried you twice, but nobody answered."

"That was you? I was afraid to answer."

"Where's Pete?"

"That's partly why I'm calling, Peggy. He's taken a quick trip to Minneapolis."

"Oh, no. Has he left?"

"Yes. Why?" Fear gripped Kyla.

"I'll go to the airport. Maybe I can catch him before he leaves. You have him paged. We have to stop him."

Kyla's heartbeat quickened and her words came out as a croak. "What's happened?"

"I finally tracked Jerald down." Peggy sounded out of breath. "Kyla, I think the hit men were in Jerald's office today."

Kyla's fingers tightened on the receiver. She dreaded what Peggy might say next.

"They took a snapshot of Pete," Peggy rushed on.

"Of Pete?" Kyla's stomach twisted another notch. "But—"

"I don't know how, but they've connected him to all this. I think they went to Minneapolis to find him."

12

PETE HAD CUT it way too close. He sprinted from the taxi to the reservation desk where the clerk waited on him with a disapproving expression. Ticket in hand, he tore up to the security check, hurried through with a prayer he wouldn't set off any alarms, and ran for the gate. He was the last person on the plane, but he made it.

Apologizing for the inconvenience, he squeezed past an overweight man on the aisle and plopped into the middle seat. Next to the window a kid listened to a Walkman and stared at the gathering twilight. The man on the aisle returned to reading the sports section of *USA Today*. Good, Pete thought. He didn't want to make small talk with a stranger on this trip.

As he buckled his seat belt and leaned his head against the tweed upholstery, he wondered if subconsciously he'd been trying to miss the flight. Telling Lillian the engagement was off wouldn't be fun, but more than that he hated leaving Kyla alone. He had to trust that she wouldn't open the door or answer the phone. If she followed those two precautions, she should be okay, but he'd learned that the unexpected was a given with Kyla.

But it wasn't just the hit men he was worried about. Some vital connection with Kyla had been broken even before he'd left. She'd walled herself off from him, maybe to spare herself potential pain.

As he considered her lack of response, another possibility occurred to him, one he didn't want to think about. One he wouldn't think about. A woman who'd made love to a man the way Kyla had to him was dead serious about the relationship, wasn't she?

Of course she was crazy about him. All he had to do was break it off with Lillian and claim Kyla's love. Right? Like burrowing insects, the fears tunneled through his confidence. Maybe she'd decided a CPA wasn't flashy enough for her. She was such a bundle of creative energy. Maybe...oh, God...maybe she'd decided life with him, once the excitement of this adventure died down, would be dull.

The concept jolted him, made him go cold. What if Kyla had second thoughts, but didn't want to hurt him by saying so? What if she'd acted that way not to spare herself pain, but to spare him?

A lurch of the plane told him they were backing away from the gate. Snowflakes spattered against the window. They looked like... Pete closed his eyes at the memory. They looked like bits of powdered sugar. In a few minutes the plane roared upward into the snow-laden clouds and pointed its nose toward Minneapolis. Pete held onto the image of Kyla being baptized with powdered sugar. No matter what happened, even if she told him to get lost, he would have that.

KYLA HUNG UP the phone and paced the room. She hadn't been able to reach Pete at the airport. Outside the bank of windows, snow had begun to fall, but unfortunately she didn't think it would be enough to ground the planes. She had one hope left. Peggy had promised to call if she caught him. They'd planned for Kyla to pick up the phone without saying anything, to protect her anonymity in case the caller wasn't Peggy. The phone hadn't rung. Kyla walked into the bedroom and checked the time on the bedside clock. The plane should be in the air by now.

Maybe Pete wouldn't go to his office or his apartment. He really had no reason to. If he went straight to Lillian's place and came immediately back to Chicago, the hit men wouldn't be able to find him...unless they'd somehow unearthed information about Pete's fiancée. Kyla forced herself not to think about that.

The phone rang and she jumped. Peggy had found Pete, after all! She curbed her excitement, picked up the receiver and held it to her ear without speaking, as she and Peggy had arranged.

"I missed him," Peggy said.

"No. Oh, no." Kyla sagged against the nightstand.

"The plane took off before I could get here."

Kyla fought off despair and straightened her shoulders. "What can we do?"

"I'll try Lillian's office and her apartment. Maybe I can alert her to have Pete lie low."

"Great. Good idea." Kyla grasped at any straw. She was ready for Lillian to keep Pete at her place all night, if necessary. The thought made her heart ache, but she had no choice. She'd do anything, suggest anything, to protect Pete. "Does he have an answering machine at his apartment? Maybe you should leave a warning on that, too."

"Good thinking." Peggy hesitated. "Take care of yourself and keep a careful watch. These guys seem really determined."

Kyla appreciated Peggy's concern. Having a friend felt good. "Don't worry. I've been taking care of myself for a long time. Besides, it's Pete I'm thinking about now. He has no idea they've identified him as the man who was with me in that office." *Thanks to your husband*, she wanted to add, but didn't out of respect for Peggy's feelings. She felt like choking Jerald T. Johnson, but without him she might be dead right now. Johnson was responsible, in a roundabout way, for her meeting Pete. Unfortunately he also seemed to be responsible for handing Pete over to the killers. "Have you filled your husband in on what's happening?"

"Yes. He's furious with me."

"With you? But he was the one dealing with mobsters."

"I know, I know."

"Peggy..." Kyla didn't continue with her thought. She was the last person in the world who should be giving advice about relationships.

Peggy sighed. "I hear what you're not saying, Kyla, and you're right. When this is over Jerald and I will have a long talk about our marriage. Some changes are overdue. In the meantime I'll do what I can to help you two. I think I should stay at the airport until Pete's flight comes in from Minneapolis. I can make all my phone calls from here while I wait."

"Okay, but contact me the minute you know something. And Peggy... do you think it's time to bring the police in?"

"Definitely not. All that would accomplish is to get you arrested. We don't know where these guys are yet. They might get away."

"Okay, but whenever you think it would help, call them. I don't care if they take me in. I want Pete to be protected, no matter what."

There was a brief silence on the other end. "You really are in love with him, aren't you?"

Kyla held her breath. *Yes.* "I . . . haven't allowed myself to think in those terms. He's engaged."

"It's okay, Kyla. He's in love with you, too. I can see it in his eyes. One of the reasons I didn't want him to marry Lillian was that he never looked at her as if he adored her. He looks at you that way."

A lump of emotion gathered in Kyla's throat. "Thanks, Peggy," she murmured. "That helps."

"You're welcome. Hang in there. Everything will work out." Then Peggy hung up.

Kyla held the phone for several seconds as the dial tone buzzed in her ear. She'd admitted something to Peggy that she'd avoided admitting to herself. Incredible as it seemed, she'd fallen in love with a man she'd met only the day before. Yet she felt as if she'd known Pete forever. The thought of a world without him in it had become intolerable.

How had it all happened so fast? And could she trust the feelings that raged through her? She gazed at the snow falling in heavy flakes past the window and was reminded of powdered sugar. *Oh, Pete.* Whether she trusted her burgeoning emotions wasn't really the issue. She was in the grip of something more powerful than she'd ever known. She had to follow where those emotions led her.

DOMINIC WASN'T HAPPY. The two seats left on the flight to Chicago weren't together, and of course Vinnie had taken the one over the wing and left Dominic back in the tail section. Dominic had studied about airplane crashes, and he knew the passengers in the tail section were a lot worse off than people sitting over the wing. Vinnie had used the excuse that he had to sit closer to the fiancée, to keep an eye on her. Sure. Vinnie always looked out for himself.

And now they were circling O'Hare in a friggin' snowstorm. All he could see out the window was white, as if the plane was covered with a sheet. Dominic shivered. The plane was covered like some stiff in a morgue.

At least the fiancée hadn't recognized Vinnie at the terminal or when they'd walked on the plane. Vinnie'd kept his hat pulled low over his eyes and pretended he was staring out the other side of the plane when he passed her row. Dominic had looked at her face and decided Vinnie had gone through too much trouble. The dame was upset, not thinking straight. She wasn't paying attention to the other passengers.

Dominic thought about his girlfriend, Suzanne, and how she'd feel if he was two-timing her. He knew what Sharon would do. She'd catch him in the act and give him a blast of rock salt in the butt with a sawed-off shotgun. Dominic didn't judge the fiancée to be the same type.

The woman on his right, next to the window, was whining about missing her connections if they didn't land soon. If they hadn't been circling ten thousand feet in the air, Dominic wouldn't have minded the wait so much. He wasn't exactly looking forward to landing. The fiancée would lead him and Vinnie to this guy, Pete, who would tell them where the girl was.

Then they'd find her, and Dominic was supposed to do the job. He didn't like the idea of shooting a girl. He liked girls. But Vinnie said this was all his fault and he had to do it. He didn't like Vinnie telling him that, but he'd probably have to shoot her, anyway. Maybe he'd put a bag over her head or something, so he could forget she was a girl when he pulled the trigger.

THE PHONE RANG again and Kyla pounced on it. She picked up the receiver and held her hand over the mouthpiece to muffle her rapid breathing.

Peggy sounded agitated. "Brace yourself."

"What?"

"I just talked to Lillian's secretary. Lillian's in Chicago. Her plane must have landed about the time Pete's took off. I raced around to see if I could find her, but no luck. I'll bet she's in a cab headed for your hotel."

"Oh, God."

"That's the bad news. The good news is I bribed the secretary with promises of cash if she'd stay at the office until Pete called. He will, I'm sure, especially if he gets no answer at Lillian's apartment. I told the secretary to tell Pete exactly what she said to me, that Lillian's making a surprise visit to her sweetheart. He'll hightail it back here. That might keep him away from the hit men."

Kyla swallowed and gripped the receiver with both hands. "Well, then, I'm glad she's come here."

"Me, too, in a way."

"I should have known she would."

"Why would you know? This is highly unusual for Lillian. She's not into surprises."

"She called here once and I accidentally answered the phone."

"Oh." Peggy paused. "So she suspects."

"I imagine that's the reason she's coming here."

"Hmm. Well, at least she won't know your room number."

"You don't think Pete called Minneapolis and gave the number to her after he checked in?"

"I doubt it. I'm sure Lillian was steamed about this trip from the beginning. They probably fought about it. I can't imagine Pete making a polite little call telling her his room number. So don't answer the phone and she'll just have to sit in the lobby and cool her heels until Pete gets here. Let him handle her."

"That's pretty cowardly on my part, Peggy."

"And you're no coward, are you?" Peggy's laugh sounded bitter. "My dear husband would have jumped at that kind of advice."

"I just think I should talk to her. This break-up isn't only Pete's doing. I'm responsible, too. I hated to send him off alone to face the music, but there wasn't any other way. Now that she's here in Chicago, I can't let him take all the heat."

"That's all very noble and good, but you're not supposed to be answering the door or the phone, except with this little system you and I cooked up. If Pete found out I'd given you the okay to do either, he'd have my head. No, you'd better stay isolated in that room until Pete gets back. It's the only way to guarantee you'll be safe."

Kyla thought up and discarded a couple of alternatives. "What if you came back here and brought her up to the room? You could use a code knock or something."

"Nope. I need to stay at the airport until Pete gets in, so I can warn him about what's going on."

Kyla sighed. "You're right. Okay, I guess Lillian gets to park in the lobby for a while."

"She'll survive. If you knew her, you wouldn't feel so guilty. The woman is a silver-plated bitch, Kyla."

"If you say so." Kyla wanted to believe that; it would go a long way toward relieving her guilt.

"I say so. Let's just concentrate on getting Pete back safe and sound. Then we'll get rid of Lillian and decide what to do about those two thugs, okay?"

"Okay."

"See you soon, with Pete in tow." Peggy hung up.

Before Kyla had a chance to gather her thoughts, the phone rang again. She knew it couldn't be Peggy, which meant only one thing: Lillian was in the lobby. With each ring Kyla felt worse. Silver-plated bitch or not, Lillian deserved to know the score.

PETE FELT as if he'd swallowed battery acid. He'd never have predicted Lillian would leave work and hop on a plane to check on him. Thank God Kyla wouldn't answer the phone or the door. Maybe they'd all be spared the nightmare of Lillian and Kyla coming face to face. But he had to get back there, pronto.

He located an overhead flight-schedule monitor and picked out the next plane bound for Chicago. Then he headed for an automated teller machine that pumped out cash up to his daily limit. He'd offer it to some passenger on that plane. Somebody who needed the money. A college student. Whatever it took, he would do it. He had to get back to Kyla.

KYLA TIMED the phone calls. They came every fifteen minutes, almost to the second. She imagined she could feel the other woman's urgency reaching up through all the floors of the hotel until it touched Kyla with waves of guilt. Kyla's agitation transferred itself to Sex, who moved restlessly around the suite and refused to settle down. Every time the phone rang Sex leaped up on the desk and meowed at the shrilling instrument as if trying to make the sound go away.

Twice Kyla had her hand on the receiver, ready to pick it up. Although she was nearly positive the caller was Lillian, it might not be. If the hit men were on Pete's trail, they might have traced him back to this hotel. They could be calling from Minneapolis, and the hotel switchboard would ring Pete Beckett's room for them, even if the desk clerk wouldn't give out room numbers. Answering the phone might put Pete in more danger than he was already in.

Kyla held the faint hope that Lillian would give up. She didn't. The phone calls, spaced exactly fifteen minutes apart, kept coming. Ten rings. The pattern didn't change. Kyla considered disguising herself and going down to the lobby, but she couldn't trust Lillian not to make a scene, and a scene would be very bad right now. The phone rang again and she clapped her hands over her ears. There had to be a way out of this. Had to be. Then she thought of one.

When the phone stopped ringing she dialed the front desk. "I believe there's a tall blond woman in the lobby who asked for Pete Beckett's room."

"Yes, ma'am," the clerk answered. "She's tried every trick in the book to get the room number, but it's against our policy. You can be assured of your privacy, ma'am."

"I'm glad to know you're so thorough. But what I'd like you to do is find that woman and give her the room number. I'm ready to see her now."

Kyla hung up the phone. She was perspiring. Peggy and Pete might not approve of what she was doing, but she had to follow her own conscience. If Pete couldn't accept that, then he wasn't the man for her.

She glanced around the suite, trying to see the place through Lillian's eyes. The double doors to the bedroom were open, revealing the unmade bed and the empty bakery box that had contained the streusel cake. Kyla rushed into the bedroom, took the box and hid it in the shower. Then she began to make the bed.

In the process of doing that she noticed a reflection of herself in the dresser mirror. She was still wearing one of Pete's shirts. Unbuttoning it, she tossed it in the closet and slammed the door. Where was her sweater? Oh, yes, she'd folded it and put it in a drawer. She flung open the drawer and grabbed the sweater as a knock came at the door. Damn! She should have done all this before she called the desk.

The knock came again. She straightened the bed as best she could and pulled the sweater over her head. Her hair was a mess and she was barefoot, but she dared not keep Lillian waiting any longer. Taking a deep breath and trying to center herself, she walked toward the door. Maybe Lillian would like a foot massage.

13

EVERY INSTINCT Kyla had told her the person on the other side of the door was a very beautiful, very poised Lillian Hepplewaite. But she had to be sure. So she peered through the peephole.

What she saw confirmed Kyla's worst fears about Pete's fiancée. Lillian's gray suede coat hung open in casual elegance. Underneath she wore a black-and-white houndstooth suit and ropes of pearls. Sleek shoulder-length hair framed an oval face enhanced with understated makeup. Kyla imagined Lillian walking beside Pete, her arm linked through his. They would be an advertiser's dream, the perfect pair to step into a new car or toast each other with a glass of champagne. Kyla couldn't fault Pete's taste.

Heart pounding, she unlocked the door and held it open just enough for Lillian to step inside. "Hurry. I'm not supposed to be doing this."

After one startled moment of hesitation, Lillian complied, bringing a swirl of expensive perfume along.

Kyla locked the door and pushed the safety latch across. Then she turned to face Lillian who, in heels, towered over her.

Lillian surveyed Kyla from head to foot. "And who are you?"

"My name's Kyla Finnegan." She stuck out her hand. Lillian didn't take it. "Pete's not here. He's—"

"But this is his suite?"

"Yes."

A white line of tension appeared around Lillian's perfectly drawn mouth. Her gaze traveled over Kyla again and remained fixed on Kyla's bare feet. Then she glanced around the room and into the bedroom, where the bed looked hastily made. Lillian glanced back at Kyla, her gray eyes cold. "I assume he's paying you?"

Kyla's mouth dropped open. "No!"

"Oh, my God, you're not even a professional. He's suckered some poor kid into giving him a last fling." Her expression was pitying. She unzipped her shoulder bag and pulled out a wallet. "Let me give you cab fare and a little something extra for the humiliation."

Kyla was beginning to understand why Peggy hadn't warmed to this woman. "I don't want any money."

Counting out twenties, Lillian glanced up. "Look, whatever he's told you to lure you up here, it isn't true. Take the money and call it a lesson learned." She held out at least a hundred dollars.

Kyla ignored the hand and the money. "Lillian, we need to talk." She kept her voice as steady as she could considering how much she longed to punch Lillian in her shine-free nose. "Why don't we sit down?" She gestured toward the sofa. At least there she wouldn't have to look up to this obnoxious woman.

"When will Peter be back?"

"That's one of the things we need to discuss." She motioned to the sofa again. "Please?"

Lillian gave her a wary look, tucked the bills back in her wallet and moved toward the sofa.

"Can I take your coat?"

"No, thanks." She sat down on the edge of the cushion, her back straight. "I see no point in prolonging this contact between the two of us. Just tell me when Peter will be back."

Kyla sat on the opposite end of the sofa. "I'm not sure. He flew to Minneapolis to see you."

"He *what*?" For the first time Lillian's reserve cracked.

"He wanted to talk to you face-to-face, about ... about the engagement. Considering how he and I feel about each other, he believes—"

"Hold it right there. You mean to tell me you think you have a *chance* with Peter Beckett?"

Kyla held on to her temper by reminding herself that in the end, Lillian would be the one hurt most. "There seems to be something very special between us, although we've known each other such a short time. We—"

"Listen, you little tart. I don't know what your game is, but I can guess what happened to Peter. He's been a little reluctant about setting the date, and now I understand. He needed to get something like this out of his system." Lillian tapped one long fingernail against the clasp of her purse. "I admit he's surprised me the past few days, first taking on this stunt of investigating his brother-in-law and now shacking up with you. Peter's always been so predictable. Guess I'll have to watch him a little closer from now on." She smiled. "Actually, this makes him a little more exciting. More of a challenge."

Kyla stared at her. "You honestly think he'd use a woman to have one last fling before he marries you?"

"I don't just think it." Lillian turned her engagement ring so the diamond caught the light. "I'm positive of it."

Kyla hadn't noticed the ring before. It was an emerald-cut solitaire of timeless beauty. Pete had chosen the ring for Lillian, or perhaps they'd chosen it together. Undoubtedly he'd told her he loved her as he'd slipped it on her finger. Was there even the slightest chance Lillian was right? No. She wouldn't believe it. "If you think Pete is capable of using a woman in that way, just to 'get something like this out of his system,' why on earth would you want to marry him?"

Lillian gave her a condescending look. "Obviously you're still clinging to some old-fashioned ideas about love and marriage, but then you're still very young. I've learned that no man is perfect, and Peter is close enough to what I want. He has a fine business going, as long as he doesn't allow himself to be distracted. This thing with his sister was insane, but maybe it was a blessing in disguise. I've sensed he was restless. This little interlude should settle him down."

As Lillian talked, Kyla felt cold all over. This woman didn't love Pete, never had. He'd come so close to chaining himself to someone who thought of him as an attractive, predictable accessory. All the passion Kyla had unearthed in him would have lain dormant. Pete's conscientious nature would have prodded him to try harder to make the relationship work, but he never could have succeeded, because Lillian didn't love him. She would have ruined his life.

Lillian stood. "Perhaps I should call his apartment and mine, to alert the poor guy I'm way ahead of him."

"He knows you're here." Kyla abandoned her concern for Lillian's feelings. This woman was an emotional danger to Pete, and Kyla would fight her off with every resource at hand. "Peggy called your office a while ago and found out you'd flown to Chicago, so she told your secretary to alert Pete when he called."

"Peggy's in on this?" Lillian's laugh was brittle. "What'd she do, introduce the two of you? I wouldn't put it past her."

"No." Kyla didn't feel like explaining.

"Then I suppose Pete will come back here. That's fine. But I suggest you pack up and leave before then. Our reunion might be a little painful for you to witness." She walked around the sofa and toward the bank of windows. "I can tell you've allowed yourself to become emotionally involved, as any young girl with stars in her eyes might—" She stopped as her gaze swept the window ledge. "What is a *cat* doing in this room?"

Kyla smiled for the first time since Lillian had entered the suite. "She's an attack cat. She belongs to me." She stood, walked over to the windows and leaned down to scratch behind the cat's ears. "And her name is Sex."

DOMINIC AND VINNIE got off the elevator arguing.

"Pipe down," Vinnie said as Dominic opened his mouth to continue. "The fiancée could be right around the corner."

"It's just not fair, you blamin' me," Dominic grumbled.

"Youse was supposed to watch her."

"I did. She wasn't doing nothin', except makin' them phone calls every fifteen minutes. Then all of a sudden, bam! She's gone, with no phone call or nothin'."

"Good thing I was playing backup and saw her get on the elevator."

Dominic glanced around. "Yeah, but there must be thirty rooms on this floor."

"We'll find the right one. You go that direction and I'll go this one. Walk slow and keep your eyes and ears open. We'll meet on the other side."

"Okay." Dominic took off for his half-circle tour.

Vinnie moved slower. He listened as he passed doors. When he heard a crying baby behind one, he mentally crossed that room off. And then a maid carrying a stack of white towels came down the hall toward him.

Vinnie doffed his fedora and put on his best smile. "Excuse me."

The maid paused and lifted dark eyebrows.

"My best buddy from high school is stayin' on this floor, but he forgot to tell me which room."

"Can't help you. Use a courtesy phone, call the desk. They'll ring his room."

Vinnie wondered what had happened to the service industry. Back when he had jobs like this, he'd tried to be polite to customers. He reached for his wallet.

"Look, mister . . ." The maid backed away.

"Just want to show you his picture, see if you remember where he's stayin'. I hate to ride that elevator all the way back down to the lobby, make the call, and ride all the way back up here."

"I don't want to look at a picture."

Vinnie took out a twenty and folded it behind the picture he held out. "Just take a second."

The maid shifted her towels to the other arm and reached for the picture and the money. She slipped the money in the pocket of her uniform before she looked at the picture. "Won't do no good. I won't recognize him. I—hey, that there's the crazy guy looking for his cat!"

"Cat?" Dammit, had the two of them kidnapped that animal out from under his nose? The thought made Vinnie crazy. The pizza. Sure. But why would anybody go to that much trouble for a damned cat?

The maid kept talking. "Yeah, the cat got away or something, but he caught it again. One of those funny kind with no tail."

Vinnie forced himself to laugh. "That's my buddy, all right. Old Pete loves that cat with no tail."

The maid peered at Vinnie with suspicion. "Said it belonged to his wife."

Wife. Had to be the girl. They were both here, in one of these rooms, with the cat. And the fiancée. Bingo.

As the maid started past him, Vinnie grabbed her arm. "You happen to know which room old Pete and the cat are in?"

She edged away from him. "No."

"Aw, c'mon. I'll make it worth your while."

"Look, mister, I really don't know. Let me alone, okay?" Her eyes were wide and she was beginning to shake.

"Why, sure. Sorry." Vinnie released her, convinced she was telling the truth. He had more than he'd bargained for, anyway. "And thanks."

Without responding, the woman hurried away.

Vinnie glanced down the hall and saw Dominic coming toward him lickety-split.

Dominic arrived, out of breath. "What happened to youse? Why didn't we meet back there?"

"Because I been here, collecting information. Guess what? They're all here. The guy, the girl, the fiancée, and that damned cat."

"The gray one?"

"What other cat we been foolin' with?"

"How'd it get here?"

"Never mind that. We still don't know the room, but here's what we do. We make the circuit again, together this time, and we listen for a cat."

"PETER ALLOWED YOU to bring a cat up to his hotel room?" Lillian regarded Sex with an expression of dislike. "The man has taken leave of his senses." She focused on Kyla again. "I return to my earlier assessment. A woman with a cat named Sex is no innocent victim of some wayward guy. What have you got going? Some videotape scheme maybe? A hidden camera in your purse with enough footage to blackmail him?"

Kyla had had enough. "I think you'd better go, Lillian. I'd planned to talk with you woman to woman about this unfortunate situation. If you refuse to believe there's any legitimate bond between Pete and me, then you and I have nothing to discuss."

"You're ordering *me* out of here? This is Peter's room. I have more right here than you do."

"I don't see it that way."

"Perhaps the manager of the hotel will. For one thing, you are harboring an illegal animal."

Kyla winced. Lillian might not end up a winner in all this, but she could do some serious damage before she went down in defeat. "I'd appreciate it if you wouldn't contact the manager about Sex."

"About Sex," Lillian cooed. "That's the other issue. I'm sure this hotel doesn't approve of guests bringing prostitutes up to the room. And that's exactly what I'll tell the manager you are."

Kyla cursed herself for ever feeling a twinge of conscience in association with this woman. "Look, let's not do anything foolish. It's a long story, but the upshot of it is that Pete is in danger. If you give away my position, you could be helping two killers find him, as well as me. So if you care about Pete at all, you'll—"

"Killers?" Lillian chuckled. "My, what an imagination you have. Now, if you'll excuse me, I'll— Damn!"

Sex squawked as Lillian tripped over her and nearly fell. Kyla wanted to laugh, but that would make Lillian even more furious. Somehow Kyla had to keep her from going to the manager. "I'm sorry, Lillian. She was sniffing your shoes. She didn't mean anything."

"I *hate* that about cats. You never know where they are."

Kyla moved between Lillian and the door. "Don't go to the manager, Lillian. Please. No matter how much you want to hurt me, wait until you've talked to Pete."

"I have you dead to rights, and you know it."

"Even if you have, do you really want to embarrass Pete this way?"

"I'd rather have you and that animal out of here before he comes back than worry about a little embarrassment. Get out of my way."

Kyla took her stance. "I can't do that, Lillian."

"What is that, some sort of martial arts maneuver? Don't make me laugh."

"I'm a brown belt. Don't push me."

"You can be a purple belt for all I care." Head high, Lillian started around Kyla.

Kyla grabbed her forearm and flipped her neatly onto her back.

Lillian's suede coat billowed out like a sail before she thunked to the carpet. She lay gasping like a beached porpoise, her face as white as the strands of pearls flung in disarray over her chest. Kyla stood ready to block her path if she tried to scramble to the door. Instead, to Kyla's amazement, Lillian began to cry. Tears slid from the corners of her eyes, leaving a damp track through her makeup. She remained prone on the floor, her eyes swimming as she looked up at the ceiling. "It's true, isn't it?"

"You need to talk to Pete."

"If it's true, I don't want to talk to Peter. Not ever again." She closed her eyes, opened them, and started to struggle to her feet.

"Can't say I blame you." Kyla held out her hand, and Lillian took it. Kyla pulled her gently upright. "Listen, I didn't start out to hurt someone. I don't think Pete did, either. I'm really sorry."

Lillian shook off her touch as if it were poison. "I don't need your pity!"

Kyla stood helplessly as Lillian pawed through her shoulder bag until she found a purse-size tissue holder. She pulled one out and blew her nose. "Let me go home," she said.

"I would, but I'm afraid you'll tell the manager about—"

Lillian shook her head. "Just let me go. I'll grab a taxi back to the airport. I don't want to be here when Peter arrives. Tell him if he has to explain, he can put it in a memo. Just let me go. Please."

Kyla had relied all her life on instincts, and now she believed that Lillian wanted nothing more than to slip away into the night. She'd been humiliated, and for a woman such as Lillian, that was the worst fate imaginable. Kyla nodded and stepped aside.

Lillian walked unsteadily toward the door. She unlatched the security bar and paused. "Tell him I'm keeping his damned ring." Then she turned the knob and opened the door.

Instantly it slammed against the wall and Lillian cried out as two men in dark suits and fedoras pushed her backward into the room and kicked the door shut behind them. Kyla recognized them immediately. A hot flush spread over her body and her feet seemed to melt into the carpet. Both men reached inside their jackets and pulled out guns.

Kyla stared at the long gray barrels, each equipped with what had to be silencers. The short beefy guy trained his on her and the skinny one leveled his at Lillian.

Lillian screamed.

"Pipe down, lady," Vinnie said in his high voice. "This'll be over quick and painless."

Lillian sounded as if she were hyperventilating. "Do something, Kyla," she gasped. "Defend us, for God's sake."

Kyla didn't reply. A curious numbness had taken over, freezing her movements, slowing her thoughts. Lillian had unwittingly led them here, of course. And bringing Lillian up to the room had played right into their hands. Peggy had been right about following Pete's instructions. But Kyla was glad she hadn't. At least Pete hadn't met these thugs down in the lobby.

Kyla wondered what a bullet would feel like going into her heart. She hoped it wouldn't hurt. Arturo Carmello seemed to die peacefully enough. *So this is how my life will end*. She thought of Trevor. Trevor would be a mess after this. Maybe Pete would be able to help her brother cope. The two people she loved most would comfort each other. She'd concentrate on that.

"Go ahead, Dominic," ordered Vinnie. "She's all yours. I'll take care of the fiancée."

"Whatever this is, I have nothing to do with it!" Lillian wailed. "Let me go, please!"

Kyla felt sorry for Lillian. She also knew it would do no good to plead. These men didn't want witnesses. Vinnie sighted down the barrel at Lillian. Kyla had the unworthy thought that maybe he'd shoot Lillian before Dominic pulled the trigger. Even seconds of life had become precious.

But Vinnie didn't shoot. "C'mon, Dominic. Get this over with."

"You first, Vinnie. I've never seen you shoot a girl, come to think of it."

"Nope. Your turn. Prove you're tough, Dominic."

Dominic sneered. *"Prove you're tough,"* he mimicked. "Why do I always have to be provin' somethin' to youse, Vinnie? Ever since we was kids I've always had to be provin' somethin'. I'm sick of it."

"Be sick of it later. Shoot her."

"I will. In a minute."

Kyla's numbness gradually wore off and a new terror gripped her. What if these two argued so long about who was going to shoot first that Pete had time to get back? She decided to goad them. She had nothing to lose. "How'd you two like the pizza I ordered for you?"

"Shut up," Vinnie snarled.

"I thought you should be comfortable as long as you were hanging out in my apartment." She noticed Dominic was listening with a curious smile on his face.

Beside Kyla, Lillian began to blubber. "Please don't shoot me. I'll pay you. I have money. I—"

"We'll take the money anyway, after we shoot you," Vinnie scoffed. "Dominic, I'm getting tired of standing here waitin' on youse."

Dominic looked at Kyla. "I liked your apartment. So youse like pepperoni, too?"

"Dominic! Cut it out!" Vinnie's gun arm began to shake as he became more agitated.

"Hey, Vinnie, there's that cat," Dominic said innocently, his eyes flicking behind Kyla.

Hysterical laughter trembled on Kyla's lips. Dominic was deliberately trying to make Vinnie furious.

Yet she didn't doubt he planned to shoot her, eventually.

"Dammit, Dominic!" Vinnie aimed at the cat.

"No!" Kyla hurtled forward, knocking aside Vinnie's arm and spoiling his aim. The shot zinged into the carpet. Kyla just had time to see Sex dart under the sofa before Vinnie grabbed her, twisted both arms behind her back and pointed his gun at her temple. In her panic about Sex she'd abandoned her karate training and reacted like any person off the street. She felt sick that she hadn't made more use of the moment, but at least Sex was safe for now.

"See what youse made happen?" Vinnie wrestled her around until they were facing Dominic. "But I ain't doin' your job for you. I'm gonna let her go on the count of three, and you'd better shoot her, or so help me, I'm turnin' this gun on you."

Dominic blinked. "Okay, Vinnie. I was just havin' a little fun. I don't like it when youse is always in charge, so I thought I'd kinda try bein' in charge. But I was always gonna shoot her. Don't get all mad. We're cousins, ain't we? Friends to the end?"

"*One*," Vinnie snarled.

Kyla noticed that no one was worried about Lillian right now. If Lillian had any guts, she could do something to distract them. But she just stood there, wide-eyed and trembling, too scared to even try an escape.

"*Two*."

Kyla wanted to close her eyes, but the barrel of Dominic's gun mesmerized her. Soon her eyes would be closed forever anyway. Pete and Peggy would find the bodies, of course. Hers and Lillian's. Poor Pete. First there were two girlfriends and then there were none. She looked at Dominic. He seemed anxious. He didn't really want to kill her, she realized, but he didn't have the courage to openly defy Vinnie, either. He'd do little things to irritate his cousin, but when it came to a showdown, Dominic would follow orders. Kyla took a deep breath. In the instant Vinnie freed her she might be able to make one move before a bullet took her out.

Then, behind Dominic, she saw the doorknob turn. Only one person had a key. Her throat closed and she almost choked as she tried to cry out a warning. "Stay away!" she managed at last. "Don't come in!"

"Oldest trick in the book, Dominic," Vinnie said, his attention trained on Kyla. *"Three!"*

As Vinnie threw Kyla away from him, the door flew open and Pete hurtled through it like a professional linebacker. Lillian screamed.

Pete tackled Dominic at the knees and the bullet from the gun whizzed over Kyla's head. The grappling men crashed into the coffee table and Dominic's gun spun out of his hand and under the sofa. The crystal vase of carnations splintered as it hit the floor.

Kyla grabbed the moment when Vinnie's attention was diverted to charge forward and chop his gun hand. With a curse, he dropped the weapon. Kyla stared in disbelief. Her karate worked!

In the instant she stood there in shock at what she'd accomplished, Vinnie retrieved the gun and aimed it at Pete.

"Pete, look out!" she cried. But the two men were tumbling in so many directions, Vinnie's gun arm wavered. Kyla moved in, grabbed his arm and flipped him before he could get a shot off. The gun flew from his grip and she scrambled for it. Vinnie reached it first. Leaping to her feet, she punted it out of his hand. The gun sailed through the huge window, shattering the safety glass. Cold air billowed into the room.

Kyla crouched, ready to attack Vinnie. Then she heard a sickening thud, and Pete groaned. She whipped around, a cry on her lips. Dominic had knocked Pete's head against a corner of the coffee table. Pete slumped forward onto the rug.

Rage swelled in her. "No!" She rushed forward and aimed a kick at Dominic's head. She missed.

Then suddenly Peggy burst through the door and barreled into the room, leaping on Dominic's back. Kyla whirled to see Vinnie fumbling under the sofa for the other gun. He howled in pain and jerked back his hand. A long bloody scratch proclaimed that Sex was still under the sofa. A siren sounded in the distance.

Dominic threw Peggy's weight off and staggered toward Vinnie. "We gotta get outta here! Cops!"

"I swear I'll kill that cat!" Vinnie ran out the door after Dominic.

Kyla started after them, but when she heard Pete groan again, she hurried back to his side. She crouched and felt the pulse in his neck. It was still strong, but he was out. Tears scalded her eyes. "Pete, I'm so sorry."

Peggy appeared at his other side. "How is he?"

"Just . . . just unconscious." Kyla sniffed. "But that's bad enough. It's all my fault, Peggy."

"Nonsense."

"I should have gone to the police right away." A siren screamed again, telling her they were coming closer. A deep-throated honking indicated an ambulance followed behind. She shuddered. "They could have killed him."

"Stop blaming yourself." Peggy turned to Lillian, who sat on the floor sobbing like a child who'd lost her favorite toy. "Hey, Lil, cut the waterworks." Lillian continued to blubber and Peggy muttered an oath. "Did you notice she didn't lift a finger? Always knew she couldn't be counted on. Always knew it. Sorry it took me so long to get up here. I was down in the lobby looking for Lillian and finally somebody told me she was already up here."

Kyla half listened to Peggy's monologue as she stroked Pete's hair. Then she realized her hand was sticky with blood. "Oh, no," she groaned, and gently parted the hair until she found where the corner of the table had cut his scalp. The blood was already clotting. It wasn't a bad cut, but the pain sliced through her all the same.

"Doesn't look too horrible," Peggy said, her voice soothing. "Heck, I probably did worse to him on the playground when we were kids."

Kyla's voice took on a hard edge. "There's a slight difference here, Peg. These men wanted to kill him." Rationally she knew Pete wasn't fatally, or even critically, wounded. He'd already begun to stir. His eyelashes fluttered and he moaned softly. Soon he'd be awake. That was no consolation as she stared at the angry red gash across his scalp.

"You were pretty handy there," Peggy said. "Was that karate or something?"

Kyla laughed bitterly. "Or something. I've never had to use it, and I let my emotions ruin my concentration. When I saw that Pete was hurt, I lost it. I was worthless at that point. Totally worthless."

"I wouldn't say that. You got rid of their guns."

"But they got away."

"And we're all still alive. You did fine, Kyla. A damn sight better than the leaky faucet sitting over there."

Kyla shrugged. Lillian's lack of courage didn't concern her, not when she considered her own foolish bravery. Worse yet, Pete wouldn't have been caught up in this insanity if Kyla had just gone straight to the police in the first place. After criticizing Lillian for not caring enough, Kyla had to face her own failings. Of course she hadn't yet fallen in love with Pete when she'd run into Johnson's office and got him tangled up in this mess. But she loved him now, and she would protect him.

The police were coming. Kyla's experience told her there would be procedures. There would be questioning. Everything would take time. And time was what they didn't have if they were to catch the men who had done this to Pete.

Vinnie and Dominic. She'd never forget their faces, and she was the sole witness to the murder of Arturo Carmello. She was the one they wanted, although they were willing to kill anyone scooped into the net with her. She had to make sure no one else was involved again, least of all Pete. Vinnie and Dominic had to be caught.

To her way of thinking, there was only one way to do that. They were more vulnerable now that they'd lost two of their guns. She didn't kid herself that they wouldn't have others stashed somewhere, but their plans had been interrupted. They'd been thrown out of their rhythm. Now was the time to set a trap.

And she would be the bait.

14

THE SIREN'S WAIL grew closer and stopped. Kyla figured it was only moments before the police and medical personnel would come barging into the room. The cops might take her into custody immediately, and she'd never have a chance to explain her plan. She had to do the unexpected and preempt them.

She spoke to Peggy in a soft murmur. "I'll walk down and meet the police. I can brief them on the situation."

Peggy looked alarmed. "On the way to the hotel Pete told me a little about your stepfather and your fear of the police. You're not thinking of running away, are you?"

"No."

"That's good. Those guys could still be hanging around somewhere, hoping to get a chance at you."

A chill slid over Kyla. What she hoped to do was dangerous, but she'd discovered that her karate really did work. She could handle things, if she kept her head. "I'm not running away, Peg. I just want to speed up this process a little."

"Okay."

Kyla eased away from Pete and rose to her feet. She hurried past a snuffling Lillian and grabbed her shoes from the bedroom.

"Sex is still under the sofa," she said to Peggy as she sat down to put her shoes on. "She'll probably stay there for a long time, but in case she comes out, don't let her get away."

"I won't, but aren't you coming right back?"

"Sure. Sure I am." Shoving her feet into the running shoes, she winced. The demands she'd put on them had left them tender, but she gritted her teeth and tied them securely. This was no time for a lace to trip her up. "Be right back," she mouthed to Peggy as Pete groaned again and started to move. Before he could come completely awake she slipped out of the door, closing it gently behind her.

The timing was perfect. A small crowd poured from the elevator—she counted four police officers, two paramedics, two hotel security guards, and a man whose three-piece suit and worried look marked him as a hotel management type. The officer in the lead apparently recognized her. He raised a hand and the other policemen stopped, their hands hovering near their holstered guns. The rest of the contingent pulled up short.

Kyla raised both hands in a defensive gesture. "It's okay. I'm not going anywhere. You'd better get the paramedics down there. A man was knocked unconscious." Saying it left a bitter taste in her mouth. "Fortunately that's the worst of it."

The officer in charge, a tall, good-looking guy in his mid-thirties, spoke. "Why don't you come on back to the room with us?" It was more of a command than a request.

"I'd like to talk to you out here alone for a minute, if I could."

He looked her over, as if deciding how much to trust her. "Harry and I will stay with her," he said to the others. "Go on down." Then he faced her, his body language making it obvious he was ready if she should try to run away. "What is it?"

Kyla spoke fast. "The men who killed Arturo Carmello just left a little while ago. I think they might still be in the area."

"We had a report from one of the guests here that there were two men racing through the halls. We have people combing the area. They'll find them."

Kyla knew how that worked. Sometimes they'd found her stepfather when he'd gone into hiding after beating up her mother. Sometimes they hadn't. Searching wasn't foolproof. "I could help you."

"How's that?"

"They want me. I was a witness to the killing."

The officer's expression remained bland. "We can talk about that down at the station."

Kyla's frustration grew. They were losing precious time because he didn't believe her. She spoke quickly. "We don't have time for that. If we act now, I can lead you to them. Here's the idea. One of you takes me down to the lobby, as if I'm under arrest. I break and run outside, like I'm being chased, and the officer runs after me, shouting for me to stop. He lets me get away. I'm pretty fast."

"Sounds like a great way to escape, Miss Finnegan. Sorry."

"I won't escape. You can have the area crawling with cops, even undercover, if hanging onto me is so important. If the two guys are still after me, they'll try to grab me, and you'll move in on them. How's that?"

The officer frowned. "Terrible." Static issued from the radio attached to his belt, and a voice crackled out a code. The officer unhooked the radio and glanced at his partner. "Watch her." He turned his back and retreated, speaking low into the instrument. Kyla could tell from the terse way he answered the communication that he was under a lot of pressure. He needed a foot massage. And he wasn't buying her plan. She should have known.

Beside her the elevator door dinged, offering her one last chance. Maybe she could seize the moment, after all. She'd had practice darting away from her stepfather enough times, but she'd never expected to be grateful for that skill. Only one of the policemen was close enough to grab her. The elevator doors slid open.

Kyla smiled at the officer beside her. "I heard the funniest thing the other day. A friend of mine named his cat Sex."

The officer looked surprised that she was making conversation. "That so?"

The elevator was wide open now. An older couple got out, and after glancing at the officers and Kyla, hurried down the hall.

On the edge of Kyla's vision the elevator started to close. She had to time this perfectly. Her palms began to sweat. "Yeah, and the cat disappeared. My friend had to run all over the neighborhood calling for Sex."

The officer smiled. The door had about eighteen inches to go. Kyla leaped.

"Hey!"

The door closed in the partner's shocked face. She'd done it! Now what? She couldn't ride the elevator all the way down. They might have someone waiting for her when she got off. She punched several buttons on the elevator, to confuse anyone who was watching from below.

When the elevator stopped at the first floor she'd punched, she leaped off and signaled another elevator. Luck was with her. It arrived empty. She hopped in, punched several buttons including the one for the lobby, and rode another five floors. Then she got off and headed for the fire stairs. She careened down them, her pounding footsteps echoing against the cement walls. She couldn't tell if someone was after her or if the echoes were from her own feet.

Panting, she hurtled down the last flight of stairs and raced for the door leading to the lobby. She paused and tried to quiet her gasping breaths enough to listen. Miraculously, no footsteps clattered down behind her.

She opened the door cautiously, her heartbeat hammering in her ears. Two policemen, their backs to her, watched the numbers lighting up beside the bank of elevators. She'd pushed a lot of buttons. She wanted them to chase her, but she also wanted a head start. She burst through the door and ran for all she was worth through the glittering lobby.

PETE WATCHED the door, waiting for Kyla to come through it. Peggy kept assuring him that she would, any minute. The paramedics had bandaged his head, and now he was answering a policewoman's questions, but most of his attention was focused on the door. Where the hell was she? Had the other officers taken her away already? If so, he wanted to know about it. He wanted to go down to the station and make sure she was okay.

Dammit, he should never have left! The heavy pounding in his head repeated the incriminating message, *all your fault, all your fault*. If he'd been here, he could have protected her better. Thank God he'd arrived when he had. The thought of what had almost happened turned his insides to ice. But where was she?

The door opened. A stern-faced cop signaled his three colleagues. "Leave this to the paramedics and the hotel security. I need you. She got away."

Pete didn't have to ask who they meant. He bolted out the door before anyone could stop him. Instinct sent him toward the fire stairs. Peggy followed him, and for all he knew, so did a cop or two. But he had ten seconds on them, and that was enough. A couple of times he thought dizziness would make him fall, but he managed to hang onto the railing and keep going. He had to. Without Kyla, his life meant nothing.

SHOUTS FOLLOWED KYLA. She knew the police were on her heels. So far so good. She spun the revolving door like a carousel and leaped into the biting cold of the night. The snow had stopped, leaving slush in the streets and on the sidewalk. She dodged a few people walking near the hotel and headed south on Lake Shore Drive. Fog shrouded the green lights of Navy Pier and the dank smell of the lake filled her nostrils. The sound of her pursuers hammered the pavement behind her, but she had a head start of several yards. A siren warbled from a distance as the backup officers were called in.

Cars whizzed along the street beside her. Panting, nearly out of breath, she scanned the area, searching for two men in dark suits. What if they shot at her as she ran? She was counting on their reluctance to do that.

Come on. I know you guys are out here.

A helicopter's rotary blades battered the air over the lake. The chopper headed her way. She'd done nothing wrong, yet the entire Chicago police force seemed mobilized to get her. Her throat ached and her legs threatened to fold beneath her. She'd never been this scared, not even when she'd run down the hall into Johnson's office.

Then they appeared. A dark sedan veered toward the curb and moved beside her.

"Get in!" ordered a thick voice.

She glanced sideways and saw that Dominic had found another gun and was pointing it at her. The helicopter's spotlight swept over her, turning the area bright as day. The police were closing in, but not fast enough. Inadequate though she might be, the success of this plan rode on her. She was exhausted and scared, but she had to perform. She cleared her mind. Then with a sharp cry she twirled in mid-stride and kicked at the hand holding the gun.

Dominic yelled as the gun soared away, and the car screeched to a stop.

"Get her!" Vinnie shouted.

Kyla balanced herself as Dominic surged out of the car. The spotlight swept over them again. Her job was to avoid getting caught, to delay them long enough for the police to move in. But she had to tease them into thinking they could capture her. If they gave up and drove off, it was the end. They'd be gone.

Dominic came toward her. His gun lay several feet away on the pavement. "Be nice, now," he said. "Vinnie's the one who wanted to shoot your cat, not me."

She landed another kick on Dominic's belly, not hard enough to fell him, but hard enough to slow him down. He grunted and kept coming. The man was a bull.

"So youse don't wanna be nice." His hands closed over her arms and she brought her knee up against his crotch. He yelled and doubled over.

"I'm leavin' youse!" Vinnie screamed, and gunned the car forward. Just then the helicopter clattered to the pavement in front of him. The wind from the blades buffeted Kyla, nearly knocking her down. In moments the car was surrounded by men with assault rifles.

It was over.

The whirling helicopter blades slowed and Kyla stood in the glare from the spotlights. She watched Vinnie get pulled from the car and pushed spread-eagle against it. Dominic was dragged up on the side closest to her and forced into the same position. They were caught. But the nightmare wasn't over.

Whoever had sent them to do the job in the first place would know who helped put them in jail. She would be a hunted woman the rest of her life.

Her legs felt rubbery and she started to sway. Maybe she'd just sit down. Maybe— As her legs buckled, strong arms caught her and she heard harsh panting in her ear.

"You crazy idiot!"

"Pete!" The spotlight drained his face of color and made his eyes glitter. He was obviously furious. But so was she. "What the hell are you doing out here?" she shouted. "You've been hurt!"

He ignored her. "You set yourself up as a decoy, didn't you?"

"And you chased out after me, with no coat, and your head bleeding!"

He shook her. "So what? You were damn near killed!"

"And you might die from a brain clot!"

"That's blood clot, you dope!"

They glared at each other until finally Kyla's eyes misted over. He was alive. The men were caught, and he was alive. Nothing else mattered. She'd go into seclusion somewhere, far from Pete, so he'd never have to be tainted by her again.

The good-looking cop she'd talked to originally walked over to them and glanced at Kyla. "Some trick."

"Some stupid trick," Pete muttered. "I think you should lock her up to save her from herself."

"I doubt we'll be locking her up, but we do need both of you to come down to the station with us and give us your statements."

Kyla took a deep breath and eased out of Pete's grip. "Could we be taken there in separate cars?"

The policeman frowned. "We can try to arrange that, if you want."

Pete glanced at her in bewilderment. "Kyla?"

She steeled herself to say it. She mustn't shake and give herself away, but this was a hundred times harder than the run she'd just made. "We've had some wild times, Pete, and some good times, but it's over. Go back to Minneapolis. I'm not sure Lillian is the one for you, but you'll find someone else, somebody suited to . . . your life-style."

She saw the blow register and looked away. What she was doing was horrible, but if hurting him now meant he'd stay alive, that he wouldn't one day be blown to smithereens by a bomb meant for her, or sprayed by gunfire aimed her way, it was worth it.

She wondered if he'd argue, almost wished he would, but he didn't. Instead he turned away, his shoulders slumped, and climbed into a nearby police car. The pain in her heart was so great she thought it might have been easier if Dominic had shot her.

TREVOR ARRIVED home late the next afternoon. Kyla had confided her fears of mob restitution to the police, and they'd agreed to keep her and her brother under constant surveillance for the next few days, at least until they had time to question Vinnie and Dominic more thoroughly. They'd examined her apartment before she'd gone back into it, and now a police car was parked across the street.

Kyla had warned Trevor, too, but he'd refused to be intimidated. He wanted time with his sister, he said. On the plane, he'd read about Kyla's exploit in *USA Today*. It took her two hours of talk and a long foot massage before she'd calmed him down a little.

"I want you to give up this business," he said, strutting around the apartment as if he were in charge. "It's too dangerous. And go into that witness protection program. God, leave it to my sister to get mixed up with the mob. You'll give me gray hairs yet, Kyla."

She smiled. Trevor's blustering was good for her right now. It distracted her a little from the void that ached within her whenever she thought about Pete. "This was a fluke, Trev. Nothing like this would ever happen again in a million years."

"Yeah, sure."

"I'll think about the witness protection program, but I'm not excited about the idea. Too restrictive." Fortunately Trevor was leaving for Detroit in three days to spend time with a buddy he'd met on board ship. Having Trevor around made her nervous, but she couldn't have turned him away as she had Pete—she was all the family he had, and vice versa. With Pete, well, she'd had dreams of being with Pete on a permanent basis. Those dreams were smashed to bits, and she needed time to mourn. Maybe after Trevor left. "Don't worry about me, Trev."

"Can't help it. It's my job." He plopped down on one of her large floor pillows and Sex jumped into his lap. She'd been skittish of him at first, but now she seemed ready to settle in with her beloved Trevor to the exclusion of Kyla.

Kyla tossed a soft kitty toy at the cat's head. "Some loyalty that cat has. I risk my neck for her and she ignores me."

"I can't believe you climbed that tree to get her away from those jerks." He grinned at her. "Well, maybe I can believe it. You were always crazy."

"Thanks, I think."

"I'd like to meet that guy Pete. Must be one righteous dude."

You don't know the half of it, Kyla thought. "He's a good person to have around in an emergency," she said, keeping her tone even. "I was lucky to run into him when I did."

"Well, I want to personally shake his hand. Might have to make a trip to Minneapolis and express my gratitude."

"Oh, I wouldn't bother." Kyla certainly didn't want that. No links.

"Wouldn't bother? Kyla, the man saved your life! You act as if he opened your car door for you or something."

"Well, it's just that he did what he had to do, and now he probably wants to forget all about it."

Trevor stroked the cat and studied her. "You fell for him."

"I most certainly did not!"

"And he dumped you afterward."

"Trevor, you have an incredible imagination."

"Runs in the family."

"Well, yours is working overtime. Pete and I are nothing to each other." Kyla jumped up and went into the kitchen. "Want something to eat?"

"Yeah. Pizza."

Her fingers tightened on the refrigerator door as she fought back tears. He *would* have to mention pizza.

Probably for breakfast he'd want streusel cake. She began to wonder if she could do this. She'd lost a gigantic part of herself and she had to pretend as if she were still whole.

"Look, if you don't want pizza, we can have Chinese," Trevor called from the living room.

Kyla took a long, shaky breath. "Pizza's fine. I'll call them."

"Okay. I think I'll turn on the news, see if you're on it."

Through swimming eyes Kyla peered at the buttons on the wall phone in the kitchen. After two tries she punched in the number of the pizza parlor. She cleared her throat and gave her order. She was hanging up when Trevor called to her.

"Come in here and listen! This is important!"

Kyla wiped at her eyes and went into the living room. She didn't need another reminder of her adventure with Pete, but she wanted to appear normal in front of her brother to avoid worrying him any more. She looked at the woman sitting behind the WGN news desk and concentrated on what she was saying.

"According to a statement issued by police, the two men accused of murdering Arturo Carmello have admitted they were hired by Carmello's wife, for the sum of two thousand dollars. Antonia Carmello was taken into custody late today, and has told police the murder was in retribution for an extramarital affair, and not the gangland killing police had first thought."

15

PETE SAT at the secluded restaurant table alone, waiting for Lillian. He wondered if she'd show. He wouldn't blame her if she'd decided to ignore his written invitation. He sipped his water and waited. A bottle of her favorite wine sat chilling in a silver bucket on the table.

She arrived a half hour late. He accepted it as her due. He watched several heads turn as she walked across the room. Without a word, she approached the table and allowed him to take off her suede coat and hold her chair. As he sat across from this attractive woman, he felt a lot of guilt.

"Hello, Peter."

He signaled the waiter to pour the wine. "I admire you for showing up."

"Well, thank you, Peter." She unfolded her napkin and put it in her lap. "I guess I have to settle for admiration at this point, don't I?"

Pete leaned his forearms on the table. "Lillian, I behaved like an ass, and I hope someday you can forgive me for it."

"Nicely said, Peter." She toasted him with her wineglass. "You did behave like an ass. But I hear through the grapevine that you're reaping the harvest from that. You ended up without either one of us."

Pete winced. Losing Kyla still hurt like hell. And now Lillian was rubbing salt in his wounds. "That's the way it should be. You and I weren't right for each other." Pete realized that, in the back of his mind, he'd been wondering if seeing Lillian again would stir up any remorse over ending the relationship with her. He felt no trace of regret.

"And Kyla?"

He figured she'd earned the right to dance at his funeral. "Apparently I wasn't right for her, either."

Lillian gazed at him and gradually the hardness disappeared from her eyes. "You know, Pete, I came here to gloat, because you really hurt my pride more than anything else and I wanted to make you pay for that."

He opened his mouth to offer another apology and she waved him into silence.

"I've done lots of thinking since that horrible night, and as much as I hate to admit it, you and I had more of a convenient arrangement than a love affair."

Pete took a deep breath. Thank God she'd said it and he wouldn't have to.

"But I'm still keeping the diamond. I'm having it made into a brooch."

Pete smiled. "You've earned it, Lillian."

She nodded and took another sip of her wine. "Now I'll confess something else to you. I'm amazed that things didn't work out between you and Kyla. She was in love with you. I could see it in her eyes when we talked in your suite. She would have done anything to protect you. Anything."

Pete reached for his wineglass and wished he had something a little stronger in it. He took a hefty swallow. "She was caught up in the romance of the moment. Once she realized she'd be stuck with a boring accountant, she backed out. Simple as that."

Lillian shook her head. "That doesn't fit my perception of the situation at all, Peter."

"Maybe not, but that's the way it is. Ready to order?"

"Of course."

Pete motioned to the waiter, who appeared at their table with menus in hand.

"I don't need a menu," Lillian said. "Just bring me the most expensive appetizer, the most expensive entrée, and the most expensive dessert you serve."

The waiter's eyebrows rose and he glanced at Pete.

"You heard the lady," Pete said, and grinned at Lillian. Then he gave his own order.

When the waiter had left, Lillian lifted her glass. "Here's to each of us finding the right person."

Pete raised his glass and drank. Except that he'd already found the right person. The trouble was, she didn't want him.

KYLA'S HANDS were damp as she stood outside Pete's office. She set down the case containing her massage oils and her tape recorder and wiped her palms on her jeans. After what she'd said to Pete the night Vinnie and Dominic had been captured, she wouldn't blame him if he threw her out. But if he did, she'd have to find a way back in. And she *would* find a way. She'd been granted her fertile mind for a reason. Winning Pete back was the best reason she could imagine.

The police had retrieved her quilted jacket and her case from Vinnie's car. Fortunately nothing had been damaged. She didn't like the fact that Vinnie and Dominic had handled her things, but she'd wiped the entire contents with a fragrant dust rag while she listened to one of her favorite tapes, to clear away the evil associations. Now they were ready for use again. Pete would be her first customer.

Straightening her shoulders, she turned the knob and walked in. A secretary, a matronly woman, looked up and smiled at Kyla. "May I help you with something?"

Kyla approved of the secretary. Her nameplate read Emma Yardley. On her desk was an ivy plant and two pictures, each of a different young family—children and grandchildren, no doubt. A wife could feel real comfortable when her husband had a secretary like Emma Yardley.

Kyla returned the secretary's smile. "I'm looking for a good accountant." She hoped to gain entrance to his office on the pretext of business. She was prepared to give a false name if asked for one. There were two accountants in this office. She knew that through her research. She glanced at the door with Pete's name on it and her heartbeat quickened.

"Both Mr. Beckett and Mr. Stripley are excellent," said Emma Yardley.

Pete sure is, Kyla agreed silently, *not even counting his abilities as a CPA.* "I believe in going by the alphabet. So I'll start with Mr. Beckett and work my way down to Mr. Stripley if necessary."

The secretary's eyes twinkled. "I'm afraid Mr. Beckett isn't in at the moment. So if you'd like to reconsider and start backward . . . ?"

Disconcerted, Kyla glanced at her watch. Where would an accountant be at ten-thirty in the morning? She'd planned this so carefully and now he was gone? "Uh, when will he be back?"

"Mr. Beckett?" Emma glanced at her own watch. "Soon, I expect. His lesson is over at ten-thirty. He has an appointment with some clients at eleven, but—"

"Lesson?"

Emma started guiltily, as though she'd committed an indiscretion. "He'll be back soon," she said more firmly. "If you care to wait, he could talk to you for a few minutes, perhaps. Otherwise I'm sure Mr. Stripley can help you."

"I'll wait."

"Would you care for coffee?"

"No, thank you." Kyla appreciated the offer and admired the hospitable atmosphere of the office. She and Pete's secretary would get along well. If they had the chance.

Kyla took off her quilted jacket, settled in a blue tweed office chair and put her case at her feet. After a brief smile, Emma returned to her word processor. Kyla glanced at the magazines on a table beside her and knew she wouldn't be able to read a word written in them. She studied her nails and flexed her fingers. Her heart kept up a rapid tattoo and her stomach felt like a washing machine on spin cycle. She hadn't counted on waiting.

And what sort of lessons was he taking? Anything to do with his job wouldn't be called a lesson. A course maybe, or a class, but not a lesson. Lessons were for physical skills like piano and tennis. She knew Pete emotionally, but there was so much about his everyday life she didn't know. So much she wanted to know.

Her last words to him had been brutal. Maybe he'd ask her to leave his office as soon as he walked in and saw her sitting there. Kyla glanced at Emma's pleasant face. Maybe he wouldn't ask her to leave because that would create a scene in front of his secretary. The thought comforted Kyla, although her stomach continued to churn. Every time the phone rang she jumped.

When the office door opened she glanced up and looked straight into Pete's brown eyes. She gripped the arms of the chair to keep from throwing herself into his arms. His familiar presence brought the memories rocketing back.

His eyes widened and he started forward eagerly, but seemed to catch himself. Turning away, he closed the door behind him carefully, as if that were the most important task in the world. When he faced her again, his expression was closed. "Hello, Kyla."

She wanted to weep at the transformation. She'd done this, made him shut down his emotional response to her. She stood, picked up her case and her jacket. "Hello, Pete. I'd like to talk with you, if you have a moment."

He glanced at Emma.

His secretary was studying them closely. "You have the Tanningers coming in at eleven."

"Kyla, maybe we should put this off until—"

"I wanted to tell you something important about Sex."

His face reddened and he glanced at Emma again. "She has a cat named Sex."

Emma rested her chin on one hand. "I see."

Pete turned to Kyla. "I don't— Oh, hell. We might as well get this over with. If I know you, you'll just keep pestering me with one thing or another until you work your way in the door."

Kyla nodded.

"Will twenty minutes be enough?"

I hope not. She nodded again.

"All right." He sighed. "Come on." He walked toward his office.

That was close, Kyla thought, following him. Pete looked wonderful. No dark circles under his eyes. Maybe he hadn't been pining for her. She hoped he had and it didn't show. She'd never seen him in business clothes. Over his gray suit and blue-striped tie he wore the trench coat she remembered so well. He carried a dark green gym bag; his lesson must have involved something athletic. He opened the office door and motioned her inside.

"Nice office." She decided it looked cozy. Pete had allowed his nature to show by choosing warm woods and burgundy leather. Outside his window a tree lifted leafless branches. In summer it would give an arbor-like softness to the view. Right now, Pete reminded her of that tree, stripped of all his softness. And it was her fault.

She scanned the paneled walls and found three landscapes and one . . . kitten? The frame didn't match the others, and neither did the subject matter. The picture was of a gray kitten with blue eyes playing with a ball of red yarn. The cat had a tail, but otherwise looked an awful lot like a younger version of Sex.

She glanced from the picture to Pete, who was hanging his trench coat on a rack in the corner. "I like the picture."

He stiffened. When he turned this time, he allowed her to see his pain. "Why are you here?"

She held up her case. "I owe you a foot massage. A really professional one. I have all my stuff back, and a deal's a deal."

"You don't owe me a damn thing. You said it all, Kyla. It was fun while it lasted, but now it's over."

"Is it?" She flicked her gaze to the picture of the kitten.

"I guess the time with you taught me I have a fondness for cats. And by the way, is there a problem with Sex, or did you manufacture that to shock Emma and get yourself in here?"

"Well, she misses having a male in her life. Both you and Trevor left. In fact, Trevor's sort of given her to me, but he thinks she'd be happier with a guy around, too. She likes men."

"Ah."

She didn't like his tone. He didn't seem quite as malleable as before. She put her case and her coat on a chair in front of his desk. She'd probably been foolish to think he'd let her massage his feet. But the case had been something to hold in her hand, something familiar to cling to.

"How's Peggy?"

"Fine."

His curt response made Kyla flinch. "Did she and Jerald work things out?"

"They're in counseling. Peggy thinks it's doing some good."

"I'm glad."

She took a deep breath and vowed to choose her next words carefully. She had to make him understand why she'd turned him away on that cold, cold night. "I suppose you've heard about Vinnie and Dominic. They were hired by Carmello's wife, not by the mob."

"I heard." He watched her, his expression wary.

"When I found out they'd only been paid two thousand dollars, I felt foolish. Here we were running from a couple of two-bit crooks."

"Who still would have killed you if they hadn't been so inept."

She tried to decide if his statement betrayed any lingering feeling for her. She couldn't be sure. "I'm just glad they didn't have far-reaching connections."

"Apparently they don't. I checked with the Chicago police and they don't think you're in any danger now."

He'd checked on her safety! Kyla drew courage from that. "Pete, I have something to—"

He glanced away. "Look, save the apologies. I figure that's why you're here." His laugh lacked any humor. "I guess I deserve this little irony. You think that what you did wasn't a very terrific way to say goodbye. Well, it was. Cut it off clean. This is what's painful, Kyla, seeing you again. I realize now it never could have worked between us, yet being in the same room with you, after—"

Panic grabbed her heart and squeezed. "You've . . . you've gone back with Lillian?"

He glanced back in surprise. "No. Why would you think that?"

"Because there were only two problems between us, Pete. Lillian was one, and the other one was—"

"I *know* what the other one was, dammit!" He advanced toward her. "I'm too blasted boring for you!"

She stared at him. "Boring?"

"Look at me!" He spread his arms wide. "I'm an accountant, for God's sake. That weekend was some sort of aberration. I don't act like that. Not ever. I don't drive getaway cars for cat-snatchers, or scoop up dirt from hotel planters, or tackle men with guns. I'm sure while I was in Minneapolis you had time to figure that out. I'm sure—"

She raced to him and threw her arms around his neck. "I'm sure you don't know what you're talking about."

He slowly lowered his arms to his sides, but didn't put them around her. "I don't?"

"Do you think I want to spend the rest of my life in that kind of danger?"

"Well, maybe not quite like that, but you're so full of energy that you seem to thrive on pandemonium, whereas I just come to the office every day. The wildest thing that happens to me is discovering a new tax loophole for a client."

She pressed herself shamelessly against him and despite his refusal to put his arms around her, he responded. He couldn't control all of him. "And after you go to the office, you go home, right?"

"Yeah, and boy, is that wild and crazy. I grab some take-out on the way home, catch a movie on TV, maybe read a book if nothing's on. Doesn't that make you drool with anticipation?"

"And then?"

"I go to bed."

"Bingo. That's where I start to drool."

He groaned and wrapped his arms around her. "You're addled if you plan to build a relationship around sex."

"Leave my cat out of this."

"Kyla . . . oh, hell." Like a man surrendering to the inevitable, he kissed her.

She kissed him back for all she was worth. She parted her lips and teased his tongue until he thrust it into her mouth with another muffled groan. He tasted like peppermint and morning coffee. She wanted to devour him.

He pulled back far too soon. They were both breathing hard. "This is ridiculous. You brushed me off once, and that was smart." He swallowed. "Okay, so we had some good times, and maybe you miss all that fun in bed, but don't put me through this, Kyla. It's not nice."

"You never let me tell you the second thing that stood between us."

"That's because I—"

She placed her hand against his mouth. "I brushed you off that night because I thought the mob would be after me for the rest of my life. I couldn't expose you to that kind of danger, so I ended it the only way I knew would work. It bothered me that you didn't argue with me, but now I know why. And your reasoning is, pardon the expression, a lot of bull. I don't find you the least bit boring, in bed or out of it."

He started to push her hand away but she clamped it more firmly over his mouth.

"Let me finish. It's true we didn't have a lot of time to sit and talk, and that's what I want now. I crave that, Pete. Sure, I've had a rough-and-tumble upbringing, and when I have to, I can act fast. But I want to learn how to act slow. I want to settle down with a man I can trust, a steady man who won't let me down. I want to have his children, plant flowers in the backyard, learn to make my own streusel cake." She took her hand away and dropped her tone to a husky whisper. "Remember the streusel cake?"

His eyes darkened. "I remember everything. Every little detail. At night I go over each second I spent with you—the awkward times, the funny times, the times when you put me out of my mind with your touch, your lips—"

"I love you."

He closed his eyes. "Do you know what you're saying?"

"Yes. Say it back."

Slowly he opened his eyes and gazed down at her with wonder. "You really mean this, don't you?"

She nodded, unable to speak.

"Oh, Kyla!" He grabbed her and spun her around the room. "I love you! And I love your crazy cat, and the way you massage feet, and your New Age music, and your brown belt in karate, and your passion for streusel cake. And for a short while I also hated you, because you showed me what life with you could be like, and then you snatched it away. I knew I'd never be content with the sort of woman I could satisfy in my present boring state, so I decided to change." He stopped spinning around and set her down again.

As she recovered from the dizzy whirl, she realized what he'd said. "Pete, no! I love you the way you are!"

"That's good to know, but that won't stop me from taking karate lessons, or learning Spanish so we can travel through Mexico and South America, or trying skydiving, or even, for that matter, becoming good at massage."

"Pete, calm down. You don't have to do all those things. Certainly not for me."

He held her tight and laughed. "Not for you. For me. You rocked me out of my rut, Kyla, and I want to stay out. I bought that picture of the kitten to remind me that life was for having fun. Peggy was right. I'm more of a man when I'm with you. Those days with you, as we risked all sorts of things, even death, I felt thoroughly, completely alive."

Kyla groaned. "What have I done? Now you'll want to try stunts that will scare the wits out of me."

"Maybe, and then when I come back from doing them, we'll make wonderful love. You can't be timid and expect to enjoy life. You taught me that."

"But, Pete, you have to think of our babies."

"Babies?" His eyes widened. "Did the condoms fail?"

"No. Future babies. Maybe even twins. They run in your family. You can't be taking risks that might deprive them of a father."

He smiled down at her. "I can't teach them to play it safe, either. That's what my parents did, and it's taken me all this time to figure out they were misguided. And incidentally, if we're going to have babies, shouldn't we think of getting married?"

Kyla's heart pounded. "If you don't think we'd be rushing things."

"Next week?"

"Perfect." She lifted her lips for another kiss. "People will call us fools for not taking more time to think it through."

His lips brushed hers. "I'd rather be happy than wise."

"Me, too." She settled herself for another long and satisfying kiss.

Partway through it Pete's phone buzzed. He reached behind them and brought the receiver to his ear as he continued to nibble on Kyla's lips.

"The Tanningers are here," Emma said.

Pete lifted his head and gazed down at Kyla. "Hmm."

When he didn't say anything more, Emma coughed. "Shall I have them wait a few minutes?"

"I need more than a few minutes for what I have in mind. Could you check with Strip and see if he could take them?"

Kyla chuckled. With a cat named Sex and a partner nicknamed Strip, Pete would have some interesting conversations in the coming years.

"I'll check," Emma said. "Hold on."

"I'm holding," Pete said, and winked at Kyla.

"Is this an important client?" she whispered.

Pete shrugged. "They have piles of money, if that's what you mean."

"Then maybe you should—"

"No." He nuzzled her earlobe. "Not today."

Emma came back on the line. "Strip will be more than happy to take the Tanningers," she said in a low voice. "He asked me to tell you he thinks you've lost your mind, blowing off a client like that."

"Then you can give him a message from me. Tell him if he's real nice to me I'll get him an appointment with my reflexologist. It's amazing, Emma. She rubs your feet, and your whole body sings. And by the way, I'm taking the rest of the day off." Then he replaced the receiver and smiled down at Kyla. "You did offer me a foot massage, right?"

She laughed. "Right."

"We'll give the Tanningers time to get settled in Strip's office, and then we'll take off for my apartment."

"In the middle of a workday?"

"My friend the kitten tells me it's the thing to do."

"And you want a foot massage?"

He looked at her, his eyes filled with love. "It's a great place to start, wouldn't you say?"

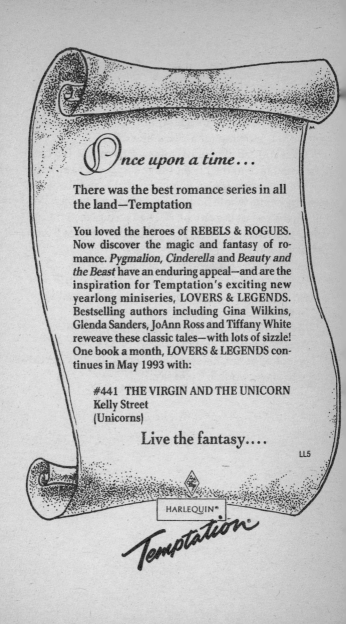

Following the success of WITH THIS RING and
TO HAVE AND TO HOLD, Harlequin brings you

JUST MARRIED

SANDRA CANFIELD
MURIEL JENSEN
ELISE TITLE
REBECCA WINTERS

just in time for the 1993 wedding season!

Written by four of Harlequin's most popular authors, this
four-story collection celebrates the joy, excitement and
adjustment that comes with being "just married."

You won't want to miss this spring tradition, whether
you're just married or not!

**AVAILABLE IN APRIL WHEREVER HARLEQUIN
BOOKS ARE SOLD**

WIN-A-FORTUNE
OFFICIAL RULES • MILLION DOLLAR SWEEPSTAKES
NO PURCHASE OR OBLIGATION NECESSARY TO ENTER

To enter, follow the directions published. **ALTERNATE MEANS OF ENTRY:** Hand-print your name and address on a 3″×5″ card and mail to either: Harlequin Win-A-Fortune, 3010 Walden Ave., P.O. Box 1867, Buffalo, NY 14269-1867, or Harlequin Win A Fortune, P.O. Box 609, Fort Erie, Ontario L2A 5X3, and we will assign your Sweepstakes numbers (Limit: one entry per envelope). For eligibility, entries must be received no later than March 31, 1994 and be sent via 1st-class mail. No liability is assumed for printing errors or lost, late or misdirected entries.

To determine winners, the sweepstakes numbers on submitted entries will be compared against a list of randomly preselected prizewinning numbers. In the event all prizes are not claimed via the return of prizewinning numbers, random drawings will be held from among all other entries received to award unclaimed prizes.

Prizewinners will be determined no later than May 30, 1994. Selection of winning numbers and random drawings are under the supervision of D.L. Blair, Inc., an independent judging organization whose decisions are final. One prize to a family or organization. No substitution will be made for any prize, except as offered. Taxes and duties on all prizes are the sole responsibility of winners. Winners will be notified by mail. Chances of winning are determined by the number of entries distributed and received.

Sweepstakes open to persons 18 years of age or older, except employees and immediate family members of Torstar Corporation, D.L. Blair, Inc., their affiliates, subsidiaries and all other agencies, entities and persons connected with the use, marketing or conduct of this Sweepstakes. All applicable laws and regulations apply. Sweepstakes offer void wherever prohibited by law. Any litigation within the province of Quebec respecting the conduct and awarding of a prize in this Sweepstakes must be submitted to the Régies des Loteries et Courses du Quebec. In order to win a prize, residents of Canada will be required to correctly answer a time-limited arithmetical skill-testing question. Values of all prizes are in U.S. currency.

Winners of major prizes will be obligated to sign and return an affidavit of eligibility and release of liability within 30 days of notification. In the event of non-compliance within this time period, prize may be awarded to an alternate winner. Any prize or prize notification returned as undeliverable will result in the awarding of the prize to an alternate winner. By acceptance of their prize, winners consent to use of their names, photographs or other likenesses for purposes of advertising, trade and promotion on behalf of Torstar Corporation without further compensation, unless prohibited by law.

This Sweepstakes is presented by Torstar Corporation, its subsidiaries and affiliates in conjunction with book, merchandise and/or product offerings. Prizes are as follows: Grand Prize—$1,000,000 (payable at $33,333.33 a year for 30 years). First through Sixth Prizes may be presented in different creative executions, each with the following approximate values: First Prize—$35,000; Second Prize—$10,000; 2 Third Prizes—$5,000 each; 5 Fourth Prizes—$1,000 each; 10 Fifth Prizes—$250 each; 1,000 Sixth Prizes—$100 each. Prizewinners will have the opportunity of selecting any prize offered for that level. A travel-prize option if offered and selected by winner, must be completed within 12 months of selection and is subject to hotel and flight accommodations availability. Torstar Corporation may present this sweepstakes utilizing names other than Million Dollar Sweepstakes. For a current list of all prize options offered within prize levels and all names the Sweepstakes may utilize, send a self-addressed stamped envelope (WA residents need not affix return postage) to: Million Dollar Sweepstakes Prize Options/Names, P.O. Box 7410, Blair, NE 68009.

For a list of prizewinners (available after July 31, 1994) send a separate, stamped self-addressed envelope to: Million Dollar Sweepstakes Winners, P.O. Box 4728, Blair NE 68009.

SWP-H493

HARLEQUIN SUPERROMANCE®

HARLEQUIN SUPERROMANCE NOVELS WANTS TO INTRODUCE YOU TO A DARING NEW CONCEPT IN ROMANCE...

WOMEN WHO DARE!
Bright, bold, beautiful...
Brave and caring, strong and passionate...
They're women who know their own minds
and will dare anything...
for love!

One title per month in 1993, written by popular Superromance
authors, will highlight our special heroines as they face unusual,
challenging and sometimes dangerous situations.

Next month, time and love collide in:
#549 PARADOX by Lynn Erickson
Available in May wherever Harlequin Superromance novels are sold.

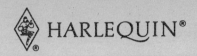